The
Fractured
Zodiac

By Ellie Burnham

ISBN: 978-1-3999-3296-7
Cover design by: Get Covers
Printed in the United Kingdom
Published by: Louisa House Publishing

Acknowledgements

Writing a book has been the most challenging yet rewarding thing I have accomplished to date, and would never have been possible without the support of the people around me.

First of all, I'd like to thank my amazing partner and the most important person in my life, Nathan, for your continuous support and belief in me. I could never have dreamed to have achieved anything like this without you being by my side. You inspire me everyday to work harder and to chase after what I really want.

I'd also like to thank Lol, Jacob and Jan - my editors. Your opinions and support has really driven me along to finish this book, and I am so grateful for your unwavering faith. Without your help, we would not have a finished product today.

My whole family has been a vessel of support and I can't thank them all enough.

And a special mention to Caroline Peckham and Susanne Valenti, two amazing authors, who not only gave me guidance on publishing but inspired me to take the leap and write this book in the first place.

Finally, of course, my dedication to Uncle Fatty.

If only I had been more aware, paid attention to the signs right in front of me.
It might have saved my life.

Prologue

The Fracturing

The ground rumbled ferociously, unleashing a beam of four elements into the clouds. A kaleidoscope of water, earth, fire, and air painted the sky. One by one, they came crashing down into the four corners of the surface, devastating whatever lay in their path.

The surface fractured into five, and with a final strike of thunder, the districts were formed.

Fire, Earth, Air and Water, each housing the now segregated zodiac signs according to element.

Mothers wailed as their children were torn from them and moved to their districts. A spell spread across Elorial, enchanting women to only give birth during their own zodiac months, triggering an onset of sudden births and a prolongation of others.

Defences rose above the ground, a towering wall of flesh-eating magma, deep enough to drown in, an enclosure of vines strong as steel, laced with poison strong enough to kill anyone who breathed the air within a mile of them, tornadoes strong enough to rip your limbs from their body, rippling with electric currents, and tremendous waterfalls, crashing down with enough power to implode any creature who swam beneath them.

Screams and wails pierced through the night sky, but found no one to listen, no one to care.

The new world had arrived.

Chapter 1

I had mere seconds to escape before I would be caught and killed.

Fear rattled through my bones as I darted beneath the water and shot towards the cliff face. I felt something snag on me but paid it no attention as I used my power to manipulate the waterfall to part, and in my haste, did not make the gap wide enough. Agony ripped through my right arm as a small amount of the falls cascaded off my shoulder.

Pushing on, I raced deeper below the surface and straight into the district centre. I darted between bodies, an unsettling amount of them stark naked, and allowed the thrumming of my heart to drive me forward.

I glanced behind me and saw a burly man with furrowed brows watching me, swimming in the same path I had just taken. My limbs turned to ice, and panic rose in my throat. I took a sharp upward turn and swam through the screams of my shoulder, the exhaustion rippling through my muscles.

I breached the surface of the water and hauled myself onto the land. I didn't stop running until I made it to my cottage and flung myself behind the door. Before I could even think about succumbing to the aches and pains pulsing through my body, I dragged a vanity unit to barricade my front door and shut all the curtains and blinds throughout the cottage.

My legs finally gave way, and I sat, panting, on my bedroom floor. Crawling to the south side of the room, I peeked between the gaps in the blinds. No one was out there that I could see, and there were no signs of disruption on the surface of the water. I felt slightly calmer at the sight, but sat there for a while more in silence, to be sure.

Eventually, my heart returned to its normal pace, and I decided I had lost them, for now. Looking in the mirror, I brushed aside my sopping wet red hair, and assessed the damage to my shoulder. My district appointed swimwear was torn down my entire right side from the hit I had taken from the waterfall. An angry black bruise snaked down my shoulder and onto my upper arm. I winced as I pulled the rest of my swimwear off and plucked out another set from beneath my bed.

The district had sent packages of them to each residence in an attempt to combat the new nudity craze that had taken over the water signs. Of course, it had changed little about the new fad, as the fae making these choices to roam nude were not doing so out of poverty, but out of 'freedom of fluidity' - supposedly our fundamental right as a water sign.

I paced across my floor, and let my mind spin into a turmoil of worries and panic.

I had started that morning the same as every other, waking to the sound of my own screams at an ungodly hour, dressing, heading below the surface into the district, and then breaking a law punishable by death by leaving the district's borders. However, the difference that morning was that I had been caught.

I had sat in the small strip of no-man's land between the Water and Fire districts, as I had done for years, when a husky voice carried across to me.

'Hey, hey, you!'

A brief glance had told me that a dark-haired man was approaching across no-man's land. I had not allowed him the chance to get close to me. If I was caught in the area, I would either be sentenced to death, which was the most likely scenario, or face imprisonment in The Centre. Seeing as The Centre was completely unattainable to reach by ordinary fae, no one knew much of what such an imprisonment would hold. However, rumours always circulated:

'All elemental powers are stripped from you,'
'Fae are forced to live amongst other elements,'
'Blood rituals are performed on prisoners,'

'The monster that defends The Centre eats uncooperative prisoners.'

So, looking at things logically, death may have been the better sentence, anyway.

I subconsciously reached for my necklace to fiddle with the crystal that hung from it, wincing as I moved my arm. Touching my necklace was a comfort I'd had since I was very young whenever I was anxious or afraid, so my heart plummeted when I felt it wasn't there. I threw myself to the floor and desperately searched through my discarded swimsuit to see if it had been pulled off. Nothing.

Crap.

Crystals were a huge part of our lives in the Water district. They held so many beneficial properties that aided fae daily. The necklace I wore had an amethyst hanging from it, refining my intuition, providing me with protection.

However, crystals weren't just to provide us with benefits, they were often passed down to children, with each generation putting a small magical signature inside it, so the family line was always with you. Fae could even access ancestral magic if they were powerful enough. This was a particularly bad thing for me, as that magical signature can be traced, and if they found the necklace, they can trace that to my parents, and therefore, to me.

It had to be back at the falls. There's a chance it might have fallen off in my hasty swimming, but that seems very unlikely, considering jewellery in the Water district was made to withstand those types of things. Besides, I had felt something snag on me briefly as I had fled.

What could I do? My mind reeled with possibilities, but the only one I kept circling back to was that I needed to go back and get it. It was risky, and most likely as good as a death trap, but either way, I would be caught now. Either they find the necklace and trace me, or I go back to get it and pray that they weren't waiting for me.

It was my only option.

I decided to wait until sunset to return, hoping anyone who may still lurk there might miss me without the full visibility of the sun. Tracing the crystal would take more than a day anyway, unless they were a particularly powerful officer.

I glanced at the clock and realised it was already 9am. I was late for work.

I worked in the district library, run and owned by an older lady, Paula, who was arguably my only friend. She was the kindest person I knew.

I dragged the vanity unit from my door, and slowly inched it open, half expecting a swarm of officers to take me away, but no such thing happened. I straightened my spine and bit the inside of my cheek, forcing myself to remain seemingly neutral and unbothered; any signs of fear or worry would alert anyone watching me that something was wrong. I observed my nearest neighbour in the distance, about half a mile away from me, also heading into the district centre in a state of hurry and found myself comforted that someone else's morning hadn't gone perfectly either.

The cobbled path slowly descended into the water, and I felt a wave of calmness and familiarity wash over me as soon as I reached it. I paused for the briefest of seconds to allow my skin and lungs to adapt to the lack of oxygen, and pushed forwards, chewing my cheek relentlessly to avoid reacting to the pain in my shoulder as I swam. Only three families lived above water, myself and two other neighbours, each about a half mile away. All buildings and facilities were under the water, our entire world was below the surface, so it made sense that most people would save themselves the hassle of going above land. But I had always felt that being on land was grounding, literally and spiritually. That, and it was the only place I could afford on my own.

I wove through the fae travelling across town and vehemently avoided the nude limbs floating around. It was surprising how much buoyancy was in the fae body, especially those of the male inclination.

I reached the library and floated through, knowing Paula wouldn't be mad that I was late. I went straight into the back office and signed in, but something in the corner of my eye snagged my attention. The lost property box.

A thought came to my mind instantly. Most fae in Water were blonde, or white-haired, yet I had striking red hair. Only a handful of families had red hair, which means it would be even easier for someone to narrow it down and identify me as the criminal.

I dug into the box and found a blonde wig, some glasses and a necklace that had a rose quartz hanging from it. I threw it all on, and looked at my reflection, which showed an ordinary Water resident, bearing no similarity to my true self.

I turned to head out into the main library, and saw Paula standing in the doorway, an incredulous look on her face.

'Well, don't you look… different?' she tried.

My steps faltered as I scrambled to think of a reasonable excuse for my appearance.

'I'm… trying out for the play?' I said, unconvincingly.

Her eyes honed in on the poster on the wall, advertising auditions for the district hall production of 'The Pirates of Penzance'. She did not look sold.

'It's called method acting,' I continued. 'If I stay in character, it will help me be a more convincing actress.'

'Yes, yes. Convincing the actress…' she mumbled. 'And it is customary to make an auditionee remove their sacred ancestral magic?' she asked, gesturing toward my imposter necklace.

I struggled not to wince as she picked up on this. Paula was so perceptive. If I had half her attention to detail, I probably would have saved myself a lot of trouble.

'You know how I feel about my parents. Forgive me if I don't feel overly attached to their power,' I lied.

Her face softened, and she didn't argue with me any further. I felt bad using her own maternal instincts against her, and I knew she didn't believe me, but it's not like I could have given her the real reason.

I headed out into the main library and tried to avoid eye contact with the rest of the staff. Not that there were many of us.

Angela Lincoln gave me a soft smile. She was a quiet, kind girl, a Pisces - like me. I knew she too was here because of her love of books and it bonded us, despite us rarely speaking to one another.

Jazlean King snorted and smirked at my appearance, and I rolled my eyes. Her and her little band of followers who worked here, who I had nicknamed The Jaz Hands, did not like me. I was essentially the deputy manager due to my close relationship with Paula, and she despised it. She came from a wealthy family, and was only made to work to be taught a lesson, unlike some of us who worked tirelessly to ensure one meal a day. She was not at the top chain of command here as she had been in school, and the lack of power drove her mad.

Last, Zachary Bloom. He waved enthusiastically at me and began heading in my direction, so I hurried away and made myself look busy.

The entirety of my shift passed in a blur, my mind never taking a pause from the constant stream of worry and the pain coursing through my shoulder unrelenting.

I noticed Paula watching me, concern blazing in her eyes as she tried to understand what was going on. I couldn't tell her, I couldn't even hint to her. Doing something that stupid once would be crime enough, let alone multiple. But my mind was made up. I needed to go back.

I signed out and left the library, keeping my disguise on to be safe. I swam under the setting sun to reach the edge of the district as fast as possible, taking care to avoid the sea creatures that were appearing now that the fae had mostly dissipated.

I went towards the edge of the district where our own elemental defence lies. There are tremendous waterfalls that would instantly slice anything that went beneath them, with the Fire district lying behind them.

However, if you swim right to the back of the district, along the border, there's a section of the falls that is thinned out enough that you can manipulate the water to ever so slightly part, just the tiniest gap, but a gap I can fit though.

Only a person with a death wish would even attempt something like it. Our powers are no match for the strength of the falls, and there's no guarantee that when you pass through the water, it won't overpower your abilities, or better yet, you'll be stuck behind the falls forever against the cliff face and die, anyway. Lucky for me, once I exert every ounce of my power into parting the water, there's a small arch in the cliff that you can pass through to reach the other side, which brings you out into the small strip of no-man's land between the Water and Fire district.

I suppose you weren't supposed to get this far at all, so little cracks in the defence, like slight arches in the cliff face, were overlooked.

Well, more fool Zephyr Oberton, because I found and exploited that weakness years ago.

I initially found the weak spot when I was told how my parents died. They were attempting to leave the district and suffered the consequences of going against the falls. I came here five years ago, at 13 years old, feeling desperate for answers to explain why they were leaving me. It was incredibly morbid, but I felt if I could just swim deep enough, I might find their bodies. Bodies which might have entailed a clue, a note, or anything that would explain their choice.

Of course, I didn't find their bodies, but in my distress, I attempted to leave the district myself. It took immense power, manipulating metres and metres of the most powerful water in the world, but it worked.

I began parting the falls, finding it especially challenging as I hadn't had time to replenish my strength. I came out the other side and hovered just below the surface of the water, my eyes scanning wildly for any movement or sign of a trap. Water stretched all the way over to the Fire district, with land scattered with debris bordering the water.

When I was satisfied that I couldn't see anyone on land or in water, I let my head breach the surface and began looking for my necklace. I went back to the point of the cliffs where I had felt it snag, and combed through all the rubble and rocks, my eyes peeled sharply for any flash of purple.

I felt his movement in the water before I heard him, but not quick enough.

'Looking for this?' asked a familiar, husky voice.

I froze, desperately trying to think of a way out. Could I make it to the arch? No. Even if I could, I wouldn't have enough power to make a hasty escape.

'I have to admit, you look slightly different from our last encounter,' he laughed. I didn't dare to turn around.

'Hey, you don't need to be afraid right now. I'm not an officer,' he said much more softly.

I almost scoffed. Did they think I was that stupid? I wouldn't fall for that trap.

My fight-or-flight instincts were in overdrive, and it seemed like fight was my only option. Training my ears for sound, I realised he was alone. I could take him. I braced myself, intending to take the opportunity when it arose.

An almost undetectable ripple in the water told me he had shifted closer toward me. Spinning around at the speed of light, I quickly took in his outstretched hand holding the necklace, his other one working below the surface to keep him afloat. I barely gave it a second of my attention as adrenaline overrode any pain and exhaustion in my body, and I lunged forward, his throat clasped in my grip, hidden by his oversized collar. His eyes widened as he realised I was striking first. I tucked my legs underneath me, and shoved my feet outwards as hard as I could, landing a blow against his stomach and causing him to double over.

As his face went under the water, I let go of his throat and grabbed his hair. I soon realised he was not a water element officer. All officers held two elements, as they were genetically enhanced, but this one did not have water; he was far too uncoordinated.

I suspected Earth - he camouflaged too well.

I didn't waste a second commanding the water to move, and dragged him below the surface. It felt barbaric, but in that moment, my only thought was to take him deep enough that he would drown. I easily deflected his flailing movements. We were underwater where I was at my strongest, though I could feel my power waning from so much use already.

I wondered why he wasn't fighting back yet. Even a non-water element could still try to incapacitate me under the water, and yet he wasn't trying.

Just as his lips started to turn blue, guilt flooded in against my adrenaline, and then his shaking hand pulled out half a journal from his pocket. I frowned. Why did he have that? He thrust it toward me, and something caught my attention on the page.

'... *a weakened spot in all defences, to allow those worthy to pass through and correct the damage done. Once the alliance is formed, only then will they find the answers they seek. It will take a great betrayal to succeed, but the doves will be set free.*

Yours Truly,

Shadow Atlas.'

I grabbed the journal with my unoccupied hand and flipped over the pages, gasping as I realised what it was. A few months after my first visit here, I found half of a beaten journal buried in the rubble on land and had read its contents so many times I could recite it word for word.

According to the journal, the author knew the Fracturing was coming, and it had been planned for years. I didn't know if the words were true, or if they were fictitious ramblings, but I had always been desperate to read the second half, to see how it ended.

This was the missing half. I looked at the man at my mercy, losing more of his life every second, and his eyes met mine, seeming to convey something incomprehensible.

Without warning, my instincts seemed to flip, and I felt a desperate need to save him. Acting thoughtlessly and driven on by my intuition, I released my hold on the water and grabbed him. I swam up to the surface with more urgency than I had ever felt, and as I looked at his face, drained of colour, panic actually seeped through me as he began to die.

I pushed myself even harder and launched his head above the surface. He took an enormous gulp of air, chased by an eruption of water from his lips. I stayed still, watching as the water in his lungs gradually made its way out of his body.

Why had I saved him? I immediately cursed myself for my lapse in judgement.

I opened the journal again, tuning out his spluttering and gasping, and flicked through the pages. The passage he had shown me matched an unfinished one in the half that I was in possession of. A quick scan through the rest of the writing told me it was all completely new entries that I had never read.

I looked up as the coughing stopped and finally dropped his collar from my hand. Panic entered his eyes once again before he caught himself and trod water. His laboured breathing was demanding all his attention right now, so I took the opportunity to study him more closely.

Admittedly, he didn't look like an enforcement officer. They were very burly and usually had a shaved head, dressed in a uniform. They float about through the district sometimes, so I'm familiar with the general look. The man in front of me was beautiful. He had tanned, olive-toned skin, a stark contrast to my ghostly complexion, and deep brown eyes. His face was chiselled and structured, as though he were carved from any woman's desire.

He wore a white buttoned shirt, with a high collar, paired with some slightly worn dark trousers. Where his clothes clung to his body from the water, I could see that his frame was quite lean, with wider shoulders, and his muscles flexed beneath his skin as he moved.

'Note to self, never take you by surprise,' he muttered, his breathing finally at an even pace.

His voice had an accent, with a more clipped tone and was well spoken. He looked up at me through the dark hair flattened to his face, his cheeks red and brows knitted together.

'Who are you? How are you here? And where did you get this?' I asked, holding up the journal.

I was still feeling sceptical about my decision to save him, but I was beginning to believe he wasn't an officer. They wouldn't be interested in something like this. And he must've known I had the other half or he wouldn't have used it to bargain back his life.

He looked as though he tried to gesture his arms toward me, but I had kept a tentacle of water snaking around him, stopping him from being able to make any attack on me whilst I was unprepared.

He scowled as he realised this.

'Get your filthy power restraints off of me. And you will answer my questions before I answer yours,' he commanded.

'Maybe you shouldn't sneak up on people without announcing yourself,' I said. 'And I'll do nothing of the sort. You don't seem to be in a position to make demands right now, do you?'

His eyes roamed up and down my appearance, his expression hard and cold and it took everything inside me not to shift back in discomfort.

'Cyrus. I'm from the Fire district. I saw you here this morning reading that journal and I put the pieces together. Quicker than you did, I might add. It took attempted murder for you to realise what was going on,' he spat.

I thought over that for a minute. He had seen me this morning, and he did have the missing half, so that was true at least. He didn't look like someone trying to arrest me, but that didn't mean that he wasn't. This could have been some elaborate scheme to entice me to say something incriminating.

'I don't know what you're talking about. I wasn't here this morning. Besides, that's impossible. Fire signs would drown in the magma before they got through,' I said, gesturing to the Fire defence.

A towering wall of magma stood opposite the falls, across no-man's land. It would melt the skin off my bones, but fire signs were impervious to temperature. The defence worked to keep them inside by making the liquid lava wall so wide and dense that they would drown in it before they were even a quarter of the way through.

'And water signs are supposed to be blown to bits swimming beneath the waterfall, but here we are,' he retorted.

I had to admit he had me there.

'Lovely to meet you, Cyrus,' I said, feeling defensive against his attitude. 'But I'm going to be going now, seeing as you're not here to arrest me.'

I withdrew the water restraining him and started to turn, trying to gauge his reaction to my rebuttal. His arm reached out towards me, fingers outstretched. I quickly knocked them away, brushing against his skin that did actually feel alien, but not before he managed to hook a finger around a blonde curl. His arm dropped to his side, and his hand suddenly burst into flames, my wig sizzling in his grip. I cursed internally and tried to play it off.

'Very pleasant. I hope you don't have a wife back in Fire. God forbid she wears a wig.' I started off towards the cliffs.

I heard a low growl rumble in his chest, and barely a second later, my arm was in the vice grip of his hand. I was too stunned to retaliate.

His skin felt like the surface of the rocks at the bottom of the ocean, smooth and sleek, but hard and impenetrable. Blazing heat emanated from his touch, not enough to hurt, but enough that it sent warmth travelling around my body like a wildfire. I glanced down at his hand. It looked the same as mine anatomically if you removed the webs and added an element of roughness. I realised he was grabbing my bruised arm, and yet I felt no pain where he touched, in fact no pain at all on my arm, only warmth.

I looked up at him in shock, only to find his face inches from mine, a similar expression on his features, a hint of awe in his eyes.

'Your skin feels like silk,' he murmured, his spearmint breath washing over my face, 'so delicate and… malleable.'

I pondered that for a moment. My skin had always felt regular to me, but I suppose it would. Delicate and silky? Maybe it was from all the time beneath the water and the constant hydration, or maybe it was because some man with rocks for fingers was the one grabbing it.

I yanked my arm backwards and scowled.

'It might feel like that to you,' - casting a pointed look at the rough skin on his hands - 'but yours feels like washed up rubble. So kindly, don't lay your hands on me again.'

That wasn't true, not even a little. His skin was almost the perfect complement to mine, soft and hard, smooth and rough, cool and warm. His skin proved he was a fire element, but I was no less suspicious of him. I decided to stop trying to flee and actually try to figure out who he was and how he got here.

A strange expression passed across his features, as though my words had actually hurt him, and he turned away.

'How are you here? And how did you get that journal?' he asked, turning back to me, his jaw set and eyes steeled.

'Me? Why don't you explain how the hell you got through the defences and explain why you were spying on me?'

'I wasn't spying!' he said. 'I saw you once. If I explain my side of things, explain yours.'

I nodded and raised an eyebrow, not liking the command in his tone but waiting for him to continue.

He sighed and fell back against a boulder beneath the water, kicking his legs to stay afloat.

'I come here a lot. When I was younger, I figured out a way to get through the magma. The journal was pretty beaten and nestled in a bunch of debris, but I found it,' I glanced over to the land on the opposite side of no-man's land, it was pretty covered in debris from when the Fracturing began, 'and I read it. Usually I come at night, but I got a feeling when I woke up this morning that I needed to be here, so I came, and there you were. I saw you reading the journal, and I soon realised it was the missing half. I genuinely didn't intend to frighten you, so I tried chasing after you to explain and found your necklace,'- he gestured towards the necklace that I had completely forgotten about in his pocket - ' so I waited for you to come back. I figured you would as there's a crystal on it, and you know the rest. A little too well,' he said, gingerly touching the bruises that were forming on his throat. 'Your turn.'

I sighed. That was horrifically un-detailed. It had given me some information: crystals must have been used in the Fire district, and he was a frequent trespasser like me. I weighed up how much truth I should give him. His story seemed to be true, but that didn't mean he was even close to being trustworthy. In fact, I didn't know why I was even still sitting there now I knew he wasn't going to arrest me.

'Similar story. I found a weak spot in the falls when I was younger, and have been coming here ever since. We haven't crossed paths before because I always come at sunrise. I found the journal buried in the sand a long time ago, and the rest is history,' I shrugged.

'That's it?'

'That's it,' I nodded.

'Well, how do you get through?'

'I don't recall you divulging those details to me,' I said. Was he really that stupid? He exuded such an energy of entitlement, as though he expected to be granted all his demands, giving nothing in return.

I suspected he was a Leo. Stubborn, seemingly powerful, and yet strangely charismatic.

'You're insufferable. How much more do I have to say before you trust me?' he asked, frustrated.

'Ha! Trust you?' I scoffed. 'You're some random guy who's appeared in an illegal area with some mystery journal, now in possession of the only proof I was here,'-

I gestured to my necklace peeking out from his worn trouser pocket - 'Do you trust me?'

'You know what? Screw you. I thought we could work together to piece together the diaries, but clearly not. You're just some Water scum, just as ignorant and vapid as I was taught you are.'

I looked at him in shock. Where the hell did that come from? This guy really had some issues.

'Okay. Well, I think that really is my cue. I sincerely hope to never see you again. Have a pleasant night,' I said in an unwavering voice, calm and levelled.

My lack of reaction seemed to anger him, and his nostrils flared in a way that almost made me giggle.

'I will take this though,' I reached toward my necklace in his hand, a small, traitorous part of me wanting to feel his skin again, 'thank you.'

He pressed it into my palm, his unblinking eyes boring into mine. I felt the smooth heat of his fingers on mine and had to work to not release a sigh. Never had I felt such warmth travel across the surface of my body before, seeking all my aches and pains and soothing them instantly. Never felt such a supportive hardness against my skin.

'It's a beautiful amethyst,' he said quietly.

He stayed there a second too long, and I jerked my hand away. Nice skin doesn't make anyone less of an ass. Without looking back, I dived beneath the water and swam straight to the ocean floor, going as deep as possible to find the weakest part of the falls. I couldn't help but notice my power was much stronger than it was when I had arrived earlier.

My heart raced as I managed to escape, still holding his half of the journal. I let out a breath of laughter and raced through to the city, the pain in my shoulder just a mere ache now.

~

I reached the city centre just as the sky turned black. Creatures of the sea now roamed freely, varying from 12ft sharks to recently hatched baby turtles. Every type of aquatic species were beautiful and purposeful in their own way, but fae and sea creatures had long since learned how to handle shared control of the water. Fae rarely stayed out after sundown, to allow the creatures their space and freedom to engage in hunting practices, and creatures had learnt not to come out during the busiest times of the day, due to poaching and our general meddling into nature's affairs.

I eventually reached The Shallows, where the water slowly ascends into land, and pulled myself out. I let my lungs readjust and the webbing between my fingers and toes began to shrink. Pulling the journal tight to my chest, I followed the stoned path toward my cottage, pushing aside the door and heading straight through to change.

I battled to get the swimwear off of my wet skin and looked in the mirror at my bruise. Somehow, it had shrunk to the size of a golf ball, and was already a green colour. I figured that the harmful magic in the falls was supposed to cause instantaneous damage, not lasting, as no one was supposed to survive.

I shivered and promptly wrapped myself in blankets to dry off. I didn't even bother to get dressed before diving into the journal in my hands. How strange that an object of parchment and ink, arguably one of the weakest substances when in contact with water, was perfectly preserved, with no smudges or tears.

I was most intrigued to see how the unfinished passage in my half connected. I had left the journal back at the falls, but that didn't matter. Knowing the words by heart, I wrote them down on some parchment and lined them up above the new passage.

'I was created to be powerful. Whilst immense power is a gift, it is a curse. No one person should house such an ability. When this reckoning descends upon us all, I shall exert every ounce of my curse into creating... a weakened spot in all defences, to allow those worthy to pass through and correct the damage done. Once the alliance is formed, only then will they find the answers they seek. It will take a great betrayal to succeed, but the doves will be set free.

Yours Truly,
Shadow Atlas.'

My mind reeled with possibilities. A weakened spot in defences? That sounds an awful lot like the weaknesses both me and Mr. Rock Fingers exploited. I'm a huge believer in fate and that nothing is coincidental, but this was testing my philosophy. There was no way there was someone more powerful than Zephyr. Even a double element guard couldn't dream of coming close to matching his power.

Of course, this was assuming this entire thing wasn't just the delusions of someone with an overly active imagination. I chewed on my lip and absentmindedly reached for my necklace, before realising I still hadn't put it back on. I rummaged through the discarded clothes and pulled it out, clasping it around my neck and removing the imposter. My mind couldn't help but briefly drift back to the way Cyrus' hands felt on mine, and I wondered how they would feel now, reaching around me and fastening my necklace that he seemed so fond of. Goosebumps rose on my skin and I shook my head, returning to my bed to carry on reading. I only imagined such things because he was so different to me biologically. As fae, he was as awful as they come, clearly riddled with issues he probably wouldn't admit, and a serious ego problem.

I turned the page and read the following lines I had only skimmed over before. These passages were all so much more brief than the ones in my half, as though the writer was more troubled, afraid.

'I fear I won't survive the week's end. It won't be long before they discover my discrepancies and hang me for it. I just hope I achieve the final ritual of my plan.

I hope to write again

Yours Truly,

Shadow Atlas.'

I flicked through a few more pages of similar words: fear of death, desire to complete a ritual, and most hauntingly, the last passage, which read:

'The ritual is complete. I have traded my mind for my body, and my soul for my life, but so long as my power lives, so does hope that the worthy ones will free the doves.

Chains and shackles will bind me after sunrise, and so I will not write again. I shall use my last drop of energy on hiding this journal to lie in wait.

Yours Forever,

Shadow Atlas.'

By the time I had inspected every entry, I was leaning away from the idea of imaginative writing. It was far too sparing on details to be the work of someone's mind, but I also could not believe someone had the power to contest Zephyr.

Zephyr Oberton was a political man, who rose into a dictatorship back when the surface was whole. He held all four elements and was the most powerful fae of all time. He became obsessed with being able to rule over each of the elements, not allowing them to interact or come together. I suppose the theory was if one of each element banded together, they are as powerful as him and thus he loses his power. Having four districts of people with enhanced abilities, however, provided him with four personal armies. He must've been incredible, in a twisted way, because his power is actually what fueled the districts. The landscapes, the defences, everything. He would have to be dead, as The Fracturing was over 150 years ago, but some powerful fae can imbue their magic into an everlasting object, so it's widely assumed that this is what he did, as we're yet to see our worlds collapse. Theoretically, if one could find the object and destroy it, the separation of the districts would dissipate, but that's impossible if you can't leave your district.

My mind swirling with a hundred thoughts, I laid down, and for the first time in years, I slept the entire night without screaming.

Chapter 2

I hid in the dark wardrobe, suffocated by all the lost and found property. A small crack of light told me someone was coming into the room.

My heart started to beat rapidly as anticipation filled me. Footsteps drew closer. I forced myself to wait for the perfect moment and then…

'Surprise!' I cheered, bursting out of the wardrobe and swimming toward Paula. 'Happy Birthday! I'm sorry it's not a cake but we both know you'd prefer this anyway,' I winked, handing her a large chocolate biscuit with an unlit candle sticking out of it.

Paula beamed at me after she recovered from her shock. 'Oh duck, you shouldn't have!' she cried, pulling out the candle and popping the biscuit into her mouth whole.

'Of course I should've. What are your plans for the day? I thought we could go to my cottage and I could try my hand at knitting again, I know you're dying to teach me,' I smiled.

Paula had been trying to teach me to knit my own blankets and throws for years, seeing as how little money I had to buy any myself, but I never really gave it the time of day.

'Oh, you do spoil me, but I'm working, chicken. You know I can't leave the library with any of those hooligans!' she gestured toward the other employees, quietly moving between the shelves.

Paula was a bit protective of her books, and hadn't had any time off in years. I was actually pretty sure she had been sleeping there, given the state of her office.

'I thought as much. Why don't you take the day off and I'll keep the place in check?' I hurried on before her protests could escape her lips. 'I promise on my eternal soul that you will return to a safe and well cared for library. You know I love these books as much as you do,' I said.

'I couldn't possibly... Could I? I suppose you do seem to have an affinity for these books. I have been wanting to run some errands and visit that new museum,' she muttered to herself. 'Oh alright, only because I trust you. This place is my entire livelihood, so if anything, *anything*, is an inch out of place, you can consider yourself dead to me, and I don't just mean metaphorically.'

She stared at me with an unwavering hardness that shocked me. I had never seen any expression close to threatening cross Paula's features before.

'Of course. I promise you, I will keep everything exactly how it is.'

A smile broke across her lips, and she leant in to peck my cheek.

Thanks, my little dove, I'm so grateful.' And with that, she scampered out the door.

My mind instantly got caught on the word 'dove', plunging me into a whirlwind of thoughts over the journal yet again. I had no idea what 'dove' was alluding to in the context of the writing, but I was beginning to realise that I wasn't going to figure it out by just staring at it.

An entire moon cycle had passed since my encounter with Cyrus, and my possession of the diary. Every day, I woke up, read my half of the journal that I had written out on parchment, went to the library and watched Paula fret over me, came home, read the second half and wrote a list of theories about where this thing had come from and what it meant. Several dead end leads had told me that, no, there is no one in history who has successfully escaped a district, no one has ever been equally, or even close to as powerful as Zephyr, and there are no books in the library which suggest anyone knew The Fracturing was going to happen before it did.

Every theory I could possibly research, I did, and every one yielded unwelcomed results. My mind had been flitting back to Cyrus occasionally, wondering if I should have found out what his take on the journal was, but considering the tumbleweed which I'm sure was blowing around on its own inside his brain, it probably would have been pointless, anyway.

I spent the day ambling around the library, very occasionally moving books to their correct homes, and avoiding Zachary Bloom.

Zach's parents and mine had grown up together, and so had we. When my parents died, his took me in until I found a foster family, and I was eternally grateful for that. Foster families were not pleasant in the Water district, as you were not given a choice. It was expected of you if you earnt over a certain threshold, and so most were not happy with my arrival. I had been to a few homes, varying in how bad they had been, but my favourite had always been with the Blooms. Which was the one of two reasons I didn't tell Zach where to stick it. He had been obsessed with me since we were early teens and had always tried to convince me to be his girlfriend. Admittedly, there was a period of time where we dated and it was nice to go through everything that comes with being a teen with someone I knew and could relatively trust.

I broke it off when I was 17 years old and had been given a district appointed property. I knew all along I did not love him. He had turned from an innocent admirer to someone who demanded much more of me. Marriage, kids and the like.

I had no interest in continuing my family line, and had lost interest in him long ago, so that was that. Except it wasn't, because he then got a job at the library too and badgered me every chance he got about getting back together. He was a Scorpio, so his determination and confidence were unwavering.

He watched me now, smiling at me every time I looked up.

I expelled a long sigh and began weaving through the library.

~

I read every single text I could find on The Fracturing and on powerful leaders in history. Truthfully, I had known Paula wouldn't spend the day with me. I just hadn't wanted her to think I was trying to get her out of the library, although I was. She had been monitoring the books I'd been reading, trying to subtly follow behind me and inspect the books I put back down on the shelves. This meant I had been trying to avoid picking up anything too glaringly obvious about what I was researching. She was a smart woman and would put it together quickly, so I needed her out of the way to allow me to read the more in-depth texts.

I sat in front of a mound of books, stacked on her desk in the office, and began reading the next book in the pile. *'Powerful Premonitions and Who Made Them'*. I flicked through the pages lazily. Most of these had been a dead end and I was beginning to bore of hunting through word by word, until a chapter heading caught my eye.

'The Fracturing: fated or just fatal?'

I hurriedly read through the introductory text, and almost fell out of my chair as I read the contents.

'A young man named Albert Kersey, a trusted seer of the Water district council, is said to have predicted The Fracturing. Witnesses claim he foresaw destruction, separation and immense power being brought to our planet, mere months before The Fracturing began. Albert was a school teacher before he became an official district seer, and claimed to have had visions even back then. Family and friends say that he always knew the weather, days in advance, and could always predict collisions and brawls moments before they happened. After his visions of The Fracturing came to fruition, he was enlisted as the district seer for the Water district council. Our journalist team sought out Albert to ask more about his premonition of The Fracturing, and see if he had any more useful insights for us, but sadly, he passed away only one short month after The Fracturing. His granddaughter, Abigail, says "Albert was a great man. Committed to doing good and helping our district. It is a shame his position on the council was so fleeting. He would have done this district a great service."'

I baulked at the information in front of me. Surely, Albert was the writer of this journal? Not only did he predict the fracturing, the 'ability' he housed must have been his gift of sight- he even predicted his own death!

'Hey, you. You do realise the time, right?' a familiar voice startled me.

'Hi, Zach. No, I hadn't realised the time. Head home and I'll lock up,' I said.

He swam out of the library and I checked out the book to take home with me, put everything else away and locked up the library for the night. In my absorption of these books, I hadn't realised it was hours past sundown.

I headed out to get home and found him still hanging around outside the library.

'I thought I could swim you home, it's dangerous when all the sharks are out,' he said with a real look of concern on his face.

I almost snorted. Sharks were not dangerous to us. Their capabilities were what was feared, despite them never attacking unprovoked.

'Sure,' I sighed, deciding not to waste my energy arguing.

He swam along next to me, rambling about how he had made it to the pro league for netball - a game where fae would fight an opposing team to score a point into a fishing net in the centre of a pitch. The object to be scored was a ball of water, and to take control of the water, you had to train to be more powerful than your opponent.

'Nice. Why do you still work at the library, then?' I asked as we stopped at the point of ascension to land.

'Well, I think you know why,' he said, a pink blush creeping into his complexion.

I opened my mouth to give him another 'friends' talk, but before I could get a word out, he leaned forward and kissed me.

I frowned as his lips moved against my open ones, still formed around the speech I was about to give. He began to pull me in close and I leaned backwards, which he did not recognise as a rejection, and instead gripped me tight and leant over me, as though we were in a dance.

I pulled out from his arms and stared at him, not sure how to react to his embrace.

He smiled gleefully and kept hold of my hand, his other hand running through his sandy blonde hair.

'I knew we would get back on track, Kaia. See you tomorrow!' he said, before swimming away.

I stayed still for a moment, unsure what had just happened, then headed up to go inside.

I let myself in and faffed around getting ready for bed, noticing that my former bruise was non-existent. I laid in the darkness, unable to stop my thoughts from going to Cyrus, and his touch.

One fleeting moment of contact had made me feel more than two years and a very demanding kiss from Zach. I slowly drifted off to sleep, imagining how something as intimate as a kiss might have felt with Cyrus if his hands on mine had felt so intense. I had no interest in finding out from a pig like him, but maybe he had a kind brother…

~

Another morning came around and I started my day to the sound of my own screams. Flashing images of blood, electric currents, and shards of ice plagued me while I slept. It had happened every night for as long as I could remember, with only one exception: the day I found the second half of the journal. It didn't even frighten me anymore, my screams often felt more like rage as opposed to fear as I had grown older.

I yawned widely. My mind had been obsessing over Albert all night. I had decided I would try to find his granddaughter today. She may be able to confirm things written in this journal, more personal passages such as *'My beautiful wife gave life to our child today. She was born with the most striking blue eyes, and the most breathtaking shade of gold on her head.'*
Small details like these could confirm whether Albert was the man I had been reading about.

I set off to feign my illness to Paula. I had been practising my cough and my weak, hoarse voice all morning. It needed to be convincing because in five years of working for Paula, I had never missed work except for school events.
Truthfully, the library wasn't work for me. I was with my only friend and able to immerse myself in an abundance of alternate worlds - a Pisces' dream.
I swam through the last straggles of reef fish, and sailed through the city centre, above the district hall where I would need to go later. A surprising number of district

council members were floating around outside the hall, and my curiosity piqued. It was quite rare to see so much activity from the council members; they tended to hide away in their underwater caves that were said to be lined with aquamarine, living separately to the rest of us common folk. I slowed and blended in with a large bush of red coral, and tried to see what had them gathering. The district leader, Councillor Marcus Asturias, and his family were just leaving the hall. My eyes widened as I realised this; the councillor, and his family by extension, never appeared in the district except to make public speeches and accept awards. They were nothing more than a figurehead, with the district running itself in day to day life.

I shifted closer to examine their appearances. I had only seen them once, many years ago, at a charity event for Scale Rot. The councillor himself was a short, stocky man, largely bulked out by a lavish short fur coat and ruffled collar. His wife was much more slight, very timid and barely looked up from her feet. She was fair skinned, and even fairer haired.

Their son was around 13 years old, very well media trained - which was now swarming -, and exuded confidence. I recognised him from his striking amber eyes. It was said that the colour of his eyes rivals real topaz itself, matching his Scorpio star sign. I had never seen topaz in person, but if his eyes were a reference, then it must have been a beautiful stone.

Then I noticed another boy trailing behind the Councillor's wife. He looked around ten years old, possibly older, but it was hard to tell from the lack of him. He was incredibly thin and had a downcast, sullen face. His eyes remained permanently trained on the ground, and he seemed to be in discomfort. His face appeared taut, as though he was trying to stop something escaping his mouth. I noticed the way his clothes did not match those of the rest of the family. They were still of rich quality, and definitely not district appointed, but they were much more worn, and didn't seem to fit properly. I found it strange that I could not remember a second son. I supposed the second son is much less focused upon seeing as he is not the heir to be councillor, less important to pay attention to and provide with luxury. What shocked me, however, was his deep brown hair. Dark hair was an almost non-existent trait in Water and the rare few who possessed it were often wrongfully judged as lesser.

So why does an Asturias hold the trait?

I watched as they swam out of the building and dodged interviewers whilst smiling at cameras as they passed by. Even the young boy seemed to have had a small amount of media training, and could deflect their questions. They headed into a roped-off area and were encircled by enforcement officers who escorted them to their cave, the enormous mansion inside just jutting out enough to glint under the sun. The luxury of the higher-ups was insane. Marcus, his wife Nia, their sons, Castor and…the other one whose name I could not recall, barely spent any time in the district, and yet owned such an extravagant home. They resided in The Centre most of the time with a smaller society that held more than one element and were also incredibly wealthy.

I pushed down my feelings of insubordination. There would be no changing this life. The rich would remain rich and the poor would remain poor. Those lucky bastards who manage to float in the middle only did so by the grace of the rich, anyway.

Continuing on my route to the library, I ran over my excuses again, ready to deliver to Paula. I headed through the main area with haste, hoping Zach wouldn't see me, and thankfully bumped straight into her.

'Oh good, Kaia, can you start organising the new arrivals, please? Councillor Asturias is back for a few weeks and we have to stock some more educational books for his children while they reside here,' Paula began.

'Paula, actually, I'm quite sick. I think I need to go home…' I choked out in my rehearsed weak voice.

'Oh, and well done you, the library was spick and span this morning. I was so pleased. What was that? You're not well? Let me look at you, ducky,' she finished before staring at me hard. 'Kaimana Green, you are not unwell. Why are you lying to me? And don't you dare lie again,' she said sternly.

Shoot.

I looked around for a scapegoat, a reason why I could leave, when my eyes found Zach's staring into mine in what was an attempt to be…seductive? Paula knew of his relentless affections for me and how I felt about that.

Perfect.

46

'Don't look now, but Zach swam me home and then kissed me last night. Like movie-style kissed, and now he thinks we're back together even though we're not, and I really need a break from him before I have to give him yet another friend-zone speech,' I whispered.

Her jaw went slack and her mouth fell into an 'o' shape. 'Is that boy on drugs? Why on earth would he even…okay, okay, no matter. Go home and come back when you can face him again, love,' she not so quietly whispered back to me.

I smiled gratefully and ignored Zach's expression, which had morphed into disappointment as I headed out the door.

I began to swim in the direction of the district hall, hoping the media would have dispersed by now. I arrived there and only a few reporters remained, so I headed inside to get the address for Abigail Kersey, granddaughter of the powerful seer, Albert.

I asked the clerk for the address and waited while she disappeared into a back office to find it in the records. As I was waiting, I overheard two reporters discussing the Asturias family.

'I know. The boy they adopted is from The Centre. Apparently orphaned, but they won't confirm or deny it. Bloody annoying when they do that. How can I write a story on maybes?' the first reporter said.

'Write it anyway, mate. Look at the kid. It has to be true. If it's not, then they'll demand it be removed from the paper for false information and then you'll have your answer,' the second one replied.

I wrinkled my nose at the audacity of the reporters. Prepared to write a potentially fake story just to get readers? How nice to know that was where our news came from.

But the information about the second son was interesting. No wonder I hadn't recognised him. How strange that they wouldn't announce their adoption and parade their act of kindness…

The clerk came back and handed me a strip of paper with an address written on it. I thanked her and left the hall. All residents were required to sign onto an electoral roll, not that elections were ever held, seeing as heirs just replaced their predecessor after death. It was more than likely used as a collation of information on us all. Family, address, age, etc. In The Centre, they allegedly had devices that told you locations, and even allowed you to communicate with another fae, just through the click of a button.

I followed the address I had been given, and arrived at a house modest in size, adorned with a show-stopping coral garden. I knocked on the door without thought and panicked as I realised I didn't know what I was going to say.

A young girl, maybe three or four years older than me, with short, blonde bouncy curls, opened the door. 'Good morning,' she chirped.

'Erm, good morning. Are you Abigail Kersey?' I asked.

'I certainly am. How can I help you?' she asked, her general perkiness taking me aback.

'Well, I'm writing a story, no, a memoir, about the memorable fae of the Water district since The Fracturing, and I wondered if you could talk about your grandfather? Albert?'

Her face began to darken, and I hurried on, anticipating her refusal. 'It's just that I read your quote in that book, *Powerful Premonitions,* and I was intrigued by him. This doesn't even have to go on record if you'd prefer?'

I hoped that my attempted professionalism made it sound as though I knew what I was talking about.

She looked at me closely for a moment before moving aside to let me swim past.

I smiled at her as she floated past me into a huge room with high ceilings, and she ushered me to sit down against a plush sea sponge sofa.

'I don't know what you're wanting to ask this time, but I doubt I have the answers. And I know you're not a journalist,' she said, raising her eyebrow at me. 'You're one of their investigators back again because you haven't got the answers you want out of *him.*'

I didn't get a chance to question what she meant by this before she stood up and picked up a small blade from the countertop. She promptly sliced it across her hand, and blood polluted the surrounding water before she fixed a vial tightly over the wound.

I was stunned. Absolutely speechless. *Was this girl mad?*

Completely caught off guard, I was compelled to drop the act.

'Are you okay?' I asked.

'I'm plenty used to it,' she said, huffing as she placed a stopper of the vial filled with her blood and handed it to me. I took the warm substance into my hand and began to protest.

'Why are you giving me this? I don't..' I trailed off as she held her hand up in my face.

'I don't know why they've sent you. Honestly, I prefer your company to those gruff men that come knocking, but you seem somewhat…unqualified,' she sniffed.

'I came to speak to you about Albert because I believe I might have his journal from before The Fracturing and wanted to confirm some details with you. You can, erm… keep this,' I said awkwardly, handing her back the blood vial. Her complexion became as white as a shell's belly, and she began to stutter.

'Y..you're not p..part of Albert's interrogation team?'

'Interrogation team? No… I live in The Shallows and have this journal'- I thrust it towards her - 'which I believe belonged to your grandfather. Why do you keep talking about him as if he's alive?'

She suddenly erupted into tears, and I stepped back, surprised. I shifted back towards her uncomfortably and awkwardly patted her back.

'Are you…okay?' I asked softly. She just shook her head as she sobbed.

I continued to pat her shoulder, providing no comfort at all, when she eventually choked out something coherent.

'I'm sorry…I thought you were…one of them,' she gasped between her tears. 'You can't tell anyone what…I just said…and did…'

'I'm not going to tell anyone. I have no one to tell,' I said.

'I largely doubt that,' she replied.

'No, honestly,' I said, trying to reassure her. 'No one likes to associate with me, anyway.'

'Why?' she asked, a hopeful tone creeping into her voice. I sighed and prepared for her reaction.

'My parents were traitors. They tried leaving the district years ago and died by the falls.'

Her head snapped up to look at me when I said this.

'Really? Do you know why?' she asked.

I really didn't like to discuss this with Paula, let alone a stranger, but I seemed to have her attention, so I thought a little truth might take me a long way.

'I don't know,' I said truthfully. ' I guess they just weren't that interested in me or in being parents.'

'Have you not used your amethyst?' she said, a quizzical look on her face.

'No? I'm not powerful enough to access ancestral magic. Even if I was, it wouldn't help me except to give me stronger powers,' I answered, not seeing the relevance. She giggled slightly.

'Oh you silly thing, were you not educated properly? Crystals don't just trace a magical signature, they store messages and memories. Anyone can store memories in your crystal if it senses that you trust them.'

'Oh…' I whispered, reeling at this new information.

Would my parents have left me a message? Could I find a way to see it?

'Do you know how to do that?' I asked.

'Of course I do! I can teach you if you like?' she asked, a blush creeping into her cheeks.

Her openness was refreshing. A fleeting doubt was quickly followed by excitement.

'Oh, wow. I mean, yes! Yes, if you don't mind, maybe there is something there…But why would you help me?' I asked.

'I know how it feels to be alone,' she sighed. 'If I had been given the chance to hear more from my family, I would have wanted to know how.'

I smiled at her gratefully, feeling an uncharacteristic ease and openness towards her, and almost forgot the whole reason I came here until she tentatively took her blood vial from my hands.

'Why did you give me this? Who did you think I was?' I asked softly.

'I think there's much about our world that you're unaware of. If you don't know something as basic as crystal magic, there's no way you know of blood magic,' she remarked, as I winced at the string of insults. 'Of course, it's because you're low-born. You wouldn't have been exposed to these types of things. I can't say much, but it's a very strong form of magic which grants additional abilities. I haven't experienced it myself, but years of exchanging blood for my life has taught me how it works.'

I remained silent, eager for her to continue. I had heard rumours of blood magic, but never had it confirmed before.

'Me and my mother have spent our lives trading our blood to…people, in order to remain alive. My grandfather you speak of, Albert, was not as popular as the textbooks would have you believe,' she finished.

'And where's your mother now?' I asked carefully, sensing I already knew the answer.

She smiled softly and held up her hand, which had wrinkles forming on the tips of her fingers.

'Her and all her sisters eventually died. Giving your blood and your magic to another in large quantities will kill you, and giving it regularly just ages you at an accelerated rate. The circle of life is quicker for this family. It's why I've never had children,' she said.

I patted her arm again, a weak attempt at sympathy.

'Why was Albert disliked?' I asked. 'He seems to have been memorialised. And why would that affect you now?'

'It's probably best if we don't discuss it. You seem kind, but I don't know you or who you work for. Albert is being punished as much as we have been, and it will only end when our line does. Anyway,' she shook her golden curls, 'you say you have a journal?'

I was about to ask why she had referred to Albert in the present tense, but she raised an eyebrow impatiently and I sensed that our conversation was over. I nodded and pulled out Cyrus' half of the journal before handing it to her.

She flicked through some of the passages, and her eyes welled with tears.

'This has to be him. He saw his demise. And the alias makes sense also. He was trying to stop anyone from publishing it most likely. Anyone who found this with his name attached could make some money by releasing it.' She trailed her fingers over the indentations in the page, feeling where the press of the pen had reflected his emotion.

I gingerly took it back from her and gathered my thoughts, feeling satisfied with that confirmation. 'Could you…I mean, would you teach me how to access my crystal?' I asked shyly, awaiting her rejection. She had most likely only made the comment out of politeness, and did not want to spend more time with someone 'low born'.

'Of course I can!' she exclaimed. 'Right, to start off with, you need to access the energies within it. Once you can feel them and harness them to your will, you'll be able to refine your intentions and direct the energy toward fulfilling them, and that includes code. Crystals have code keeping qualities which store spiritual messages to be passed along.'

I nodded eagerly, not really understanding what she said, but wanting to learn.

'Close your eyes, and place your fingers around the crystal,' she said in a low, mesmerising voice, and I did as she said. 'Focus on the texture of the crystal, feel the ridges beneath your touch and the coolness of the surface. Now, feel deeper. Feel the personal connection you have to your crystal, and think of the guidance it has given you, the protection.'

I felt what she said, and thought of the tingles I get when I'm in danger, or not sensing something I should. I thought of how my necklace was my comfort and provided me with a sense of safety and security.
'Now, envision the energy flowing from the crystal into your fingertips,' she continued. 'Feel the coolness seep into your skin, and feel the thrum of energy rippling through your hands, slowly spreading along your arms.'
I felt a cool buzz spread along my arms, shoulders, and hands.
'I feel it,' I whispered.
'I can see,' she laughed.
I opened my eyes and saw that water was swirling all around me, ever so slightly pushing her furniture in a circular motion.
I smiled and let go of the crystal, feeling energised.

We said our goodbyes and set the intention to meet again so she could teach me how to use the energies to my will. I left her house, intending to swim straight back home before the sun fully set. But a feeling in my gut just kept nagging at me, and I realised what it was I needed to do.

Chapter 3

I sat against a sandy bank in no-man's land, watching the sun go down. I knew Cyrus liked to visit this place at night, and I had to admit it was mesmerising to watch the golden rays of the sun bounce off of the water. It could never truly be dark here, not with a towering wall of blazing heat only a few metres to my left. The swirls of magma danced around one another as I walked toward the Fire defence and I watched in awe. I couldn't see through to the other side, it was far too wide, but I wondered what it must look like to withstand such a blazing heat. I felt an urge to reach out and touch it, but instead restrained myself to just hovering my hand close enough that it began to burn.

'I wouldn't touch that if I were you,' a voice came from beside me.

I turned to find Cyrus paddling in the water slightly to the right of me, towards the small strip of land.

The orange glow of the sun suited him. It made his skin shine and shadows fell across him in a way that perfectly contoured his face.

'I wasn't going to. My hand is beginning to burn from this distance,' I replied, drawing my hand back in toward me, noticing a blister had begun to form. 'I dread to imagine what would happen if I made contact with it.' Without warning, he plunged his entire arm into the lava, and I struggled to stifle a scream. He chuckled and drew it back, completely unharmed.

'I didn't think you'd come here again, not once you escaped with my half of the journal,' he said accusingly.

'Honestly, neither did I. But I thought about what you said, *before* you called me ignorant and vapid,' I said, raising an eyebrow. 'I agree we at least need to hear each other's theories about this thing to make it make sense, because I think I know who it belonged to.'

His head snapped up to look at me and his hard gaze made it hard to maintain eye contact.

'What? How? Who?' he questioned.

I didn't respond immediately, trying to think of the best way to handle this situation with him. He wasn't trustworthy by any means, but he was the only one who knew about it, about anything.

In my hesitance to answer, he darted forward out of the water and grabbed my shoulders. I tensed up defensively against the heat now spreading through me and balled my fists. His arms drew me in closer toward him, and I breathed in the scent of spearmint, leather and smoke.

'Tell me, now. This is more serious than you could ever know,' he pressed.

'Okay…I will. But I want more answers from you first. I'm confiding in a man that has fewer manners than a pig and you seem to think you're entitled to my thoughts, so I would like some of yours first,' I said, shaking myself out of his grip. Instantly, the heat left my limbs, and I found myself wishing it hadn't. He grumbled under his breath and ushered me to follow him. He dropped onto the sand and looked up at me.

'You can stay out of that water. I'm not having you do that thing with your hands and drown me again if you don't like my answers,' he scowled.

He failed to realise I could still control the water to come and grab him and take him down, but I felt that pointing out more murderous tactics I had was not the best way to win his trust.

'Who are you, really who are you? How do you get through?' I asked, remaining standing.

He sighed and seemed to study me. His eyes roamed from my expression, down my body and took in my position. His eyes met mine, and he spoke in a rough voice.

'I get through because there's a weak spot. The lava streams that run through the district often spit out onto the rocks and slate. It is usually majorly overlooked as we can't feel it anyway, but a few years back I noticed one particular area that seemed to spit almost mechanically. Every three seconds, a fist sized splash of lava flies out of the stream and lands in the same spot. I watched it for a few minutes, and realised despite that much heat hitting against the surface, the ground wasn't burning or forming small craters like it should.' He looked at me to ensure I was still following and then continued. 'I wondered if that area of rock was a type of mineral or crystal that maybe hadn't been discovered, and was harder than the other substances in the district. So I used the full force of my powers on it, and unsurprisingly, it crumbled away. I paid it no attention after that, assuming I had been mistaken, and carried on about my day. But when I passed by it again the following evening, I noticed the spitting was still like clockwork, and the ground had managed to heal itself. There was no trace that I had done anything to it at all. I used my powers again, and it fell apart as it had done previously, but this time I didn't walk away. I lit a flame and looked below the rubble to see a tunnel. I went down and followed it through. It led me to what I believed was a dead end, but I thought of the entrance and how it had needed strong power to reveal it, and so I used my flames on the dead end, and a rush of water flooded through. I got carried out by the conflicting currents, and ended up in this strip. Now each time I want to go here, all I have to do is blast the entrance and exit, and they seal themselves up as soon as I've passed through so no one can follow,' he finished.

I was amazed at the descriptions of his district. It sounded like an alien, dangerous place, but also intriguing and exciting. I was also impressed that his power had managed to uncover the weakness. Overall, it was actually a very similar story to mine.

'What about you?' he asked. 'What's your name and how do you get through?'

I figured I owed an explanation after he granted me his. 'At the edge of the district, right in the back corner, the falls seem to run thinner. I was…in the area…and I was trying to leave the district. I used my power along the falls to no avail until I reached one spot, where the water fell so thinly I could gain control of it. I parted it aside and there was a small arch way behind it. I swam through and it took me right to the edge of the falls, that backs on to this strip of land,' I explained, avoiding his eye in case he queried my reasons for leaving the district.

'My name is Kaimana Green,' I said, finding myself compelled to tell him that information.

'So what have you found out?'

I explained how I had discovered Albert Kersey, everything Abigail had briefly told me about blood magic, and how she had alluded to him being alive, only leaving out the part about crystal magic. I noticed Cyrus had laid back on his elbows and unbuttoned his shirt, leaving his midsection to glisten in the last remaining rays of sunset. His eyes were shut, and I took the chance to scan over his body before swallowing thickly and averted my eyes from the muscle running up and down his abdomen.

'Albert had a vision, something immediately after The Fracturing, and has never revealed what it was. Abigail says they're all being punished, including Albert. She seemed to think I was an official from The Centre, after her blood,' I finished, anticipating the same shocked response I had given Abigail earlier.

However, when I looked back toward Cyrus to gauge his reaction, he hadn't even bothered to open his eyes, let alone show any trace of shock or confusion.

'You aren't surprised by this…' I whispered, a knot forming in my stomach.

He blew out a large breath of air and sat up to look at me. His eyes were steeled, and I felt as though somehow I had said something wrong.

'No,' he responded darkly.

'Why?' I asked warily.

He let out a low grunt and fastened his shirt. The sun seemed to have disappeared, a dark fog settling across no-man's land, and the momentary complacency I had felt in his presence vanished.

An overwhelming urge to slip into the safety of the water consumed me, and I trusted the instinct. I slowly dropped down into the shallows of the water in front of the strip of land, still facing Cyrus.

He watched my movements carefully, and his shoulders tightened in defence. He shifted onto his knees, his hands outstretched inches above the ground.

We stared at each other for a long moment, his dark eyes holding incomprehensible secrets.

His fingers twitched, and I felt watched as the smallest tendril of smoke drifted from them. Without thinking, I created a vortex of water to rise myself above him. I held the water, ready to make a defensive strike to pull him under, but found myself plummeting downwards instead. Cyrus had emanated a trailing blaze from his palms, the fire varying shades of orange and red. It hit my tower of water, creating a hissing steam when it made contact. The vortex evaporated, and I tumbled into the burning steam, cursing as burns brushed against my skin.

I dived and swam down to the very bottom of the seabed, and used the sanctuary of being immersed in water to funnel all my strength into a wave, making it rise above the surface and feeling it engulf Cyrus. I closed my eyes and focused on the energies rippling through the water, and found Cyrus' tumbling a few metres in front of me. I darted forwards and gained control of him, wrapping tentacles of water around his arms and legs and rendering him immobile.

He tried to thrash against the tentacles, to no avail. He finally saw me in front of him, and tried to blast fire straight at me, but instead of flames, a surge of bubbling, boiling water came crashing towards me and I lost my grip on the tentacles as I recoiled in pain.

He started swimming madly toward the surface and with a trembling hand, I pulled him towards me once more. My power was shaky. I was in my element, which made me much stronger than Cyrus, but I was hurt. Blisters of heat spread along my arms, part of my chest and the side of my neck.

He came barreling towards me, and I quickly parted the water to make a pocket of air on the sandy floor. We both crumpled onto the floor, panting, Cyrus coughing up more water, reminding me of our first meeting when my mistrust of him had yet again been replaced by benevolence.

I reprimanded myself internally for my weakness. I'd had him completely at my mercy, again. Why had I bothered granting him oxygen?

He barely wasted a second before encircling me with flames, but just as I stretched my arm out to bring the water crashing back down, he called out.

'Wait! Just…wait. I'll lower the fire if you stop trying to kill me. You realise this is the second time now? My lungs are beginning to get used to the feeling of being filled with water,' he gasped.

I didn't trust him, especially not when he had me trapped in a ring of fire, but I still had the upper hand by having the water completely surrounding our pocket of air, and could let it fall any moment. Plus, I needed to try and conserve some of my energy to heal my wounds, or I wouldn't be able to fight back at all.

I nodded, and dropped my arms by my sides. Instantly, he dropped the flames. It surprised me that he was so quick to extinguish them completely, considering he was the most vulnerable right now.

'Why do you do that? It seems like everything is fine and then you freak out and try to kill me! Last time, I understood. You were frightened, didn't know who I was. This time proves you're just barbarous. I was just sitting there!' he yelled, his voice deep and angry.

'You're right, I didn't know who you were. And I still don't. You clearly are involved in some dark business. I could tell by your reaction to what I told you. Besides, you went to strike first,' I retorted, not yelling the way he had done due to the pain coursing through me.

'I struck first? You're mad. You're delusional! I suppose you think I was also trying to attack you the day I approached you, don't you?' he laughed, cruelly.

I thought I had controlled my expression, but evidently I did not.

'I knew it. What's wrong with you? I was just sitting there, thinking how to explain what I know, and before I had the chance, you were slinking off into the water and creating some absurd whirlpool, trying to pull me under!'

I stayed silent for a moment. He saw things very differently from me. I began to doubt whether he really had been about to attack, or whether it had been me being far too impulsive and presumptuous.

'You sat up, and you looked angry and your hands were smoking, ready to fight…' I trailed off quietly as I realised how ridiculous that sounded aloud.

'Oh! I see! My hands smoked, so you try to drown me. I'm a fire element!' he cried.

His tone made me feel defensive, and my body tightened up, bracing for him to lash out.

He stopped pacing across the sand in anger and stared at me. He did nothing but this for about 5 minutes before I cleared my throat, his gaze making me feel oddly vulnerable, as if I were naked. His eyes trailed over my forming burns and something similar to guilt overtook his features.

He suddenly strode toward me and gripped my arms. My hands automatically unclenched, ready to strike, but he slid his hands down my arms and gripped them tightly.

'Stand still,' he said, glaring into my eyes.

I complied, and relaxed my hands, finding it hard to resist the comforting warmth that was now travelling through my body. My mind was screaming at me to move. Escape. But my body remained as still as stone.

His smooth skin brushed against mine, slowly travelling from my hands up towards my shoulders. I noticed that I no longer felt the burning pain, despite the fact Cyrus' hands were almost as warm. I looked down and saw that where his fingers trailed, a soft glow emanated, my burns healing behind it.

I turned my eyes toward him and found him to be looking at me already. I forced myself to hold his gaze and found myself leaning in to him ever so slightly. Why was it that his general presence was untrustworthy, unsettling, and yet I seemed to be unable to keep myself away? I should have killed him twice over now, or at the very least ran and never looked back. But here I was.

His spearmint breath washed over me again, and I closed my eyes as I inhaled the scent. Why was it that a smell relatively unfamiliar to me felt so comforting?

His hands reached the top of my shoulders and slowly trailed sideways, skimming over the blisters on my chest. I felt the warmth of his presence draw closer to me, and I opened my eyes once again. His eyes were fixed on where his fingers were gliding across my collarbone and down toward the neckline of my swimwear. His other hand reached up and cupped my neck, and I stopped myself from leaning into it.

How could I trust a man who can go from causing these burns to caressing them in mere minutes? Something didn't feel right.

I pulled backwards, and he clearly disagreed with my movement as he gripped my arms tightly by my sides. I wrenched my shoulder free and placed my hand firmly on his chest and pushed backwards, and he let go of me instantly.

He looked at me with a guarded expression, his dark hair messy and tousled from our fight.

'Who are you? What do you know about The Centre?' I asked harshly. I wasn't going to be fooled into trusting someone who had just been attacking me, even if his warm skin held some mysterious healing magic. He was only prepared to use it on me because he had just inflicted those same burns.

'Do you thrive on animosity? Do you wish to live in a state of chaos?,' he said, his eyes dark and angry. 'I know everything you told me, Green, because my name is Cyrus Rayos.'

I didn't get to reprimand him for the use of that nickname, because I was stunned into silence by his admission.

'Rayos? As in…Fire district leader Rayos?' I stuttered.

'Yes. My father is Reginald Rayos, the leader of Fire. So, yes, I have heard everything there is to hear about The Centre and I know about many types of forbidden magic, blood rituals included. I think your theory about Albert is possible, so I need to get to The Centre and find out.'

Without speaking, I moved our pocket of air through the water, taking us up to the surface. We broke through the water and silently swam to shore. I sat on the sand, finally feeling as though I didn't need to be ready to fight for a few moments.

It all made sense, his strong power, his aura of entitlement, and the fact he seemed to know so much about everything before I did.

The only thing I didn't understand is why he felt so strongly about Shadow Atlas, or Albert, and especially not why he felt the need to go to The Centre.

'Why?' I said at last. 'Why do you need to go to The Centre? How would you even get there and why is this journal important to you?'

'Look, it's pitch black out here now, and it's going to be noticed that I'm missing; I'm usually always home by the time the sun has fully set. It's a long story, and I will explain it to you, if I can believe I can trust you,' he said sternly, looking into my eyes.

'Trust me? Have I not laid myself out on the line to come here?' I asked incredulously.

'Meet me here tomorrow, at 6am sharp, and bring a copy of the Water district's resident ledgers. If you bring it with you, then I'll know I can trust you. It's illegal to take them outside of the district buildings. Oh, and try to kill me again and I will have to fry you to ash,' he said, ignoring my protest. He dived below the water and I watched him swim down to what I could only imagine was the entrance to his district, and he slowly faded out of view as the darkness of the depths overcame him.

I felt frazzled. What had I done? Somehow, I had tried multiple times to incapacitate the Fire district heir, someone extremely powerful and involved in dark magic, who knew my full name and my criminal activity. No wonder he wasn't as defensive as me. He could probably get away with breaking a law much worse than leaving the district.

I chewed on the inside of my cheek as I headed to the waterfall and parted my way through. It was almost effortless, and I couldn't help but wonder if Cyrus' healing magic had somehow also made me stronger.

I swam through the district and arrived home, my cheek now a bloody mess thanks to my incessant biting. I had no idea what to do, but it didn't seem I had a choice.

I had to break yet another law at the will of the Fire heir.

Chapter 4

I decided I had become too complacent around Cyrus.
I should have continued to press for his identity, or better
yet, not gone back and engaged in another dance of death
with him. I didn't know what his presence did to me, but
I needed to be stronger against the effects. It was
probably some charisma charm placed upon him so the
district adored him as much as Reginald. Lest they have a
mutiny on their hands.

He had put me in an uncomfortable spot. I could refuse
to return and not add another crime onto my growing
list, but he could easily whistle blow to his father and
have me arrested. Of course, he would incriminate
himself also, but I highly doubted that mattered to him.

I rolled over in bed and realised it was already 4am. Two
hours before I was due to meet Cyrus. I dragged myself
out of bed and sat before my vanity unit, wondering how

I was going to hide the fact I hadn't slept due to my agitated state.

I tossed aside my hair, not bothering with it as it would soon be wet anyway, and instead focused on trying to reduce the puffiness from my face. I didn't know why I was even bothered, it's not like I had anyone to impress, but I was more vulnerable than ever and it felt like a last ditch attempt to make me appear to have some semblance of control.

I used some sea kelp scrub and applied some essence of pearl moisturiser, and my skin definitely looked revived. The tiredness beneath my eyes wouldn't go away so easily, so I gave up and got dressed.

I headed over to my wardrobe, only to find in my absentmindedness over the past months, I had not done any washing. Usually, this wouldn't matter, I had around 50 swimsuits, but all that was left in the maple wood unit was a pile of red ones. They were like the others, with a V neckline and shorts on the bottom, except these were an illuminating red, with long sleeves instead of short.

I groaned and pulled one on as I had no other choice, but I could already feel the stares coming my way.

Water signs generally always wore blue or white, and I was already different due to my hair being a vivid red. Now I would be even more of an anomaly, looking like a walking candy cane with the way my pale skin contrasted the colour of my suit and my hair. I shook my head before leaving the house. No point in moping over it.

～

70

I reached the district hall and felt sceptical that it would even be open. According to my watch, it was 4.53am, and there were still sharks, whales and even reef fish, the most wary of them all, out swimming, indicating that the fae had not awoken yet. I swam up to the towering double doors, and gently pressed against one, for it to swing open and grant me entry. I raised my eyebrows in surprise and swam through.

The desk was empty, and I began to feel hopeful that this would not actually be a very difficult task after all. I hurriedly made my way over and peered through the doors into the back office. I couldn't see anyone and so decided to hop over and grab the ledger, a huge black file that I could see behind the office doors.

The doors refused to open, and I realised there was a keypad next to the handle. Of course they were locked. Why would they leave these documents out for free pickings? How on earth would I do this now?

I looked all around the desk, hoping to find a slip with the code on, or maybe a key. I found no such thing, but I did hear commotion outside and so made my way over to the double doors.

Outside, there was already a bundle of reporters forming, which was not a good sign. I glanced at the time on my wrist. 5.15am. I was slowly losing time to get the ledger and make it to Cyrus on time, but I saw no way to get to it.

A sudden onslaught of flashing cameras sounded, and I looked back out of the doors to see the Asturias family heading this way. I cursed and slipped outside, hoping to blend in with the reporters, ducking low and getting amongst the central throng to keep my red hair and suit unnoticed amongst the reporters attire as best as possible. Thankfully, all of their gaze was firmly directed one way.

'Thank you! Thank you!' Marcus' voice boomed, although there was no applause. 'Now, we're here today to announce the adoption of our beloved son, Alastor. He is an orphan from the Central Island, and we have taken him in to provide him a loving home, and become part of the most powerful district.'

I almost scoffed. Most powerful? We were third in rank in terms of power, with the order going Air, Fire, Water then Earth.

I did, however, find it interesting they announced this adoption.

'I have invited you select few here to be the ones who publish this story, and I am pleased to hand over my son, Alastor, to answer your questions,' Marcus continued.

This piqued my interest. I was curious about what he had to say, and see if he seemed at all pleased about this adoption.

His sunken face suddenly brightened, as if the smiling features had been painted on, and he stepped forward, somewhat shakily.

'Good morning, fellow water residents. What questions can I answer for you?' he asked. His voice shocked the reporters; he lacked the softer spoken expression of water elements, and instead his voice was hoarse and strained.

'Alastor, what's your power level?' one reporter shouted.

'Alastor, over here, please! How do you feel about being adopted by Marcus Asturias?' another called.

Several more questions shouted toward the boy, and I noticed that this did not break his facade at all. He was well trained.

'My power level is yet to be determined. As you are aware, all heirs are ranked against one another to determine the district's power level when they are in leadership. As I have only just become the second heir to the Water district, I have not yet undertaken the necessary tests. I am ecstatic to have been adopted by my mother and father, and already feel brotherly love toward Castor,' he smiled.

'What happened to your parents, Alastor?'

The question rang out and silenced all the other reporters, everyone hanging on to hear what the response would be.

Alastor's smile faltered, and he seemed to become confused.

Marcus quickly stepped in and steered him away from the reporters, into Nia's arms, who had been standing by unobserved in the background.

'Alastor's parents were brilliant, upstanding residents of the Central Island, and they unfortunately passed away from a nasty case of Web Disease, which unfortunately spread through the webbing of their fingers and toes and the infection caused their demise. This is why we will be donating half a million lunas to the Web Disease Foundation.'

It sounded plenty generous, and it was, but I read once that district council leaders earn a million lunas per week, it wasn't exactly a hardship to them.

I noticed a small movement out of the corner of my eye and saw that the clerk had opened up the office by this point, and was peeking surreptitiously out of the doors to listen to the press conference. It was my only opportunity.

I casually swam inside and floated about, pretending to look at the memoirs on the wall, and waited until she finally braved going outside, into the sea of reporters to better hear what Marcus was now proclaiming. I shot through the office doors and smiled to myself when they flung open at my push. Quickly scanning the files on the shelves, I grabbed the one labelled 'District Contact Registration'.

I made my way out of the office and behind the desk just as she came back inside, still glancing over her shoulder at the councillor's family.

She looked at me in surprise, her short blonde curls bouncing as she gasped.

'Oh! What are you doing back there? What do you have in your arms?' she exclaimed.

I had no idea what to do and decided to just make a break for it. If I stayed I would still be caught, so I thought I may as well try my luck.

I darted forwards, almost knocking her sideways, and flew out of the doors. Weaving through the sea of reporters, I hoped she would lose sight of me, and I could hear her shouts getting fainter and fainter and thought she may have given up. But when I turned around, two enforcement officers were swimming toward me with grisly faces.

I panicked and started swimming toward the library, hoping I could get there first and disguise myself like I had before. However, enforcement officers are genetically enhanced, and unfortunately for me, one of them held the earth element. A huge wall of sea vines formed in front of me and I took a sharp upward turn to swim above it. As soon as I was over it, it disappeared, and sharp pieces of coral shot out towards me, growing speedily from the seabeds, trying to block my path. I dodged them as best I could, taking a few scratches to my arms in the process. Glancing behind me again, I realised they had gained on me massively, despite my haphazard swimming. I tactically crashed into a group of naked fae and dropped the ledger. A mental note of where it had landed formed in my mind, and I watched as the guards hesitated before squirming to push through the naked limbs.

I felt hands gripping my swimsuit and thought they had already got to me, but then realised it was just some freedomists encouraging me to join them. I looked in horror as numerous body parts waved and bounced against me and hastily shoved through them all before they managed to undress me.

I saw Zach swimming toward the library and dashed over to him.

'Zach!' I called.

'Oh, hey, babe. I've been wondering where you've been. You went home from the library the other day and Paula said you felt nauseous,' - well, I suppose that was true - 'so I stopped by your place to bring you some cold coral soup, but you weren't home. I waited about two hours before I headed back. How come you were out so late?' he asked, brows furrowed.

I bit my tongue to refrain from telling him to mind his own business, to stop coming to my house and to remove his arm that had slid around my shoulders.

I opened my mouth to begin a lie, but before I could, the large, stocky enforcement officers caught up to me and tugged my shoulder.

'Excuse me, ma'am, do you care to explain why you were attempting to escape from the district hall?' one asked in a gruff voice.

I widened my eyes and pretended to look confused. 'Escape? Oh, I would do no such thing! You see, I had heard that Marcus Asturuis was doing a press conference, so I headed that way to see if I could catch a glimpse - I'm just such a huge fan - but then I looked at the time and realised I was late for work! That's when I ran into Zach here, who works with me. Isn't that right?' I smiled sweetly at Zach.

'Errr…' he stuttered.

Come on, Zach, do one thing right.

'Well, yeah, that's right, I mean we work at the library and…err…yeah,' he got out.

Phew.

'Library doesn't open until 9am, girl. Come with us, please,' the guard grunted.

Damn it.

He placed his hand on my arm and began to tow me behind him. I started trying to think of a way out of it when I was suddenly pulled backwards and out of his grip.

'If you don't *mind*, we have been asked to open up the library early today because the Asturias children are having a study session at 9am and we need to prepare for their arrival! Now, please stop manhandling my girlfriend and let us get to work,' Zach said sternly.

I stood, shocked, and looked towards the guards to see their reaction to this. They looked at each other, and mumbled between themselves.

'...I did hear that they're staying a while...'

'...is it worth the risk? She doesn't even have anything...'

Eventually, they looked between us and nodded, grunting something about making our way.

I smiled in amazement at Zach, realising he had just prevented my arrest.

'Wow. Thanks, Zach. How did you think of that so fast?'

'Because that is what we're doing, isn't it?' he said, puzzled.

'Oh, I mean, yes, but I'm not actually getting there too early because I have some plans with...a new friend of mine, Abigail. So, I guess I'll see you later?' I replied, having no idea we were supposed to be opening early today.

'Sure thing, babe,' he winked, and gave my cheek a very sticky kiss.

I frowned, and was about to tell him we weren't dating, but he had already set off swimming, whistling as he went.

I shook off the encounter and looked at the time. 5.58am. I was going to be late, but Cyrus would have to suck it up. I was already unhappy that I was acting on his beck and call like a bottom feeder, but I wanted more information out of him, and I wanted to hear his truth. I swam back to where I dropped the ledger, half sticking out of a coral bed, the freedomists having dispersed.

～

By the time I reached the falls, I was very late. I paused before heading through, realising I didn't know why Cyrus had such an interest in the Water district records. I skimmed through it and realised it had residents dating back to the formation of the district, up to the present. I looked through for my own name.

Kaimana Green

2 The Shallow Gardens

No Contact Information

Next of kin: Lilith Green [deceased]p2063 , Arthur Green [deceased]p1918

Age on year of DL (District Ledger) Renewal : 18

I frowned as I read this. I had no idea that so much personal information was just laid out for anyone to request.

I flipped the page to page 2063. The page that contained my mother's name. Her entire passage was written in red ink, different from almost all the other residents listed.

Lilith Green
DECEASED AND DISREGARDED
Prior residence: 54 Harbour Passage
No contact information
Next of kin: Arthur Green [deceased]p1918, Kaimana Green p3520
Death: Age 36, implosion by District Waterfalls

I flinched as my eyes travelled over the word 'disregarded'. It was the term used for traitors.

I tore out my mother and father's pages, not wanting Cyrus to see what they were.

I pushed through into the clearing of no-man's land at 7.31am, and saw him sitting on the small strip of land, his back facing me. I smirked to myself and sent a silent torrent of water up behind him before dumping it over his head.

He jumped to his feet and created a ball of blistering heat that encircled him. Flames covered the entirety of his skin and burned viciously.

I cackled as I drew nearer, but slowly stopped as I got a closer look at his power. He had turned to face me and his eyes were a vivid red, and the cage of heat that trapped him was mostly clear, with a small ripple of heat running through it. Ultra thin tethers of fire stretched across it, looking like lightning in their own right.

Orange and red runes flashed over the surface of his creation, but none that I recognised.

'What the hell is that?' I whispered.

His gaze met mine and flashing images of screaming, blood, and terror raced through my mind.

I staggered forwards and saw my own mother being dragged and beaten as my father hurled frozen shards of water towards someone I couldn't see. I heard my own voice screaming, and blood covered my hands.

My vision slowly returned to me, shrieks still echoing in my ears, and I wobbled in the water. I looked at Cyrus in bewilderment, seeing he was still producing some type of dark magic. I encompassed him in water, pushing against his own defences.

I felt the resistance of his powerful magic, and could feel my reserves getting low after using so much to pass through the falls.

My control over the swirling water began to wane, and Cyrus' fire was growing stronger and stronger.

I thought back to my brief lesson with Abigail and placed one hand on my amethyst pendant. I focused as much concentration as I could spare into feeling the energy inside the crystal. It felt calm and light, like a gentle ray of sunlight in the midst of a storm. I opened myself up to receive the energy, and the cool feeling flowed through my fingers, slowly spreading across my entire arm. I let it travel into my other hand and then exerted it into the magic I was creating with it.

The water suddenly seemed to come alive, and tentacles shot from all directions, pummeling into Cyrus' cage of heat.

One managed to break through and landed on his feet. With the breach in his magic,the other shots of water made it through much easier and extinguished the flames on his body as they hit him.

He crumpled to the floor, and I stopped wielding the water.

I dropped beneath the water for a moment, trying to push the images I had been shown from my mind and regaining some strength.

Eventually, after taking a long breath and regaining my composure, I moved forward and floated in the water a few metres away from Cyrus. I waited for him to speak, but the only noise he made for a long while was the sound of his shallow breathing and a faint sizzling noise which seemed to be coming from his skin.

'Do you have it?' he finally asked, gruffly.

'What?'

'Do you have…the ledger?' he growled slowly, talking to me as though I were unintelligent.

I realised I had dropped it in my attempt to push back against his attack, and dived beneath the water without a word. I swam to the approximate place I had been when the visions started and reached the ocean floor.

It was sitting, half sticking out of the sand, the pages I tore out a few yards behind it, tumbling through the turmoil of the falls. I took the ledger and left the pages down there to be washed away forever.

I broke the surface and raised it in front of me.

'Yes. I have it. You, however, aren't getting anything until you explain what just happened,' I answered.

He only looked at me from under the soaked curls on his forehead with blazing fury and said nothing.

'What did I see? Is that real?' I whispered.

'What exactly would that be?' he replied coldly.

'My parents…they were being attacked, and I was covered in their blood…'

He laughed darkly, and I looked at him in shock.

'Lucky you. I don't know if that's real or not, but I know what I see is,' he muttered.

'What was that magic? Those runes…' I trailed off, his expression telling me to stop talking.

His eyes were still a simmering orange, and I could have sworn there were actual flames dancing behind them. He stepped into the water and kept himself afloat, inches from my face.

'I'm in the water. You have the upper hand and I can't create flames. Now that you're in control, give me the ledger,' he commanded, his voice cold and cutting.

I despised the way he spoke to me, totally disregarding the entire show he had just put on, which was, without doubt, some dark, dark magic.

'Why would you assume I want control? You know nothing about me.'

'You are always the first to attack. You won't leave your element unless it's on your terms. You have shown up here over an hour late to keep me waiting for you and exert the control you have over me. You are yet to hand me the whole reason I even care to see you and continue to demand more information than you are entitled to,' he said furiously.

I paused before responding. He seemed to have a point. 'You're wrong about why I'm late. It wasn't deliberate. There was a press conference at the district hall and I couldn't get by unnoticed,' I argued, pointlessly.

'Why was there a press conference before 6am?' he asked, his anger momentarily placated.

'Marcus and Nia Asturias have adopted a new child from The Centre and they were giving some reporters the exclusive,' I answered, unsure why he cared.

He clearly became impatient and took the ledger from my hand, careful not to touch me.

He flicked through it quickly, settling on the pages dedicated to the Asturias family and read over the information which had already been inputted for the adopted son.

Alastor Asturias
1 Canyon Cave
No Contact Information
Next of kin: Marcus Asturias p1 , Nia Asturias p2
Age on year of DL (District Ledger) Renewal : 12

Siblings recorded: Castor Asturias p1

I noticed that none of the other residents had their siblings recorded, and I presumed this was a stark reminder that Castor was still the prevalent son, and most important as the next heir.

He then flipped to a page which held Albert Kersey's name, and I cursed internally for not looking at that first.

Albert Kersey
DECEASED
Prior residence: 76 Coral Gardens
No contact information
Next of kin: Marigold Kersey [deceased]p234, Lillian Kersey [deceased] p879
Death: Age 87, lung deflation

I read the information upside down, interested in seeing the names of next of kin, but otherwise did not see how that provided more information than I had already gathered.

He continued flipping pages until he reached one which had been torn out. My father's.

He looked up at me and frowned.

'Where is this page, Kaimana?' he demanded.

I resisted the urge to shift uncomfortably and held his gaze.

'I don't know,' I said simply.

He growled again, and his nostrils flared, which made my mouth twitch into a smirk. Poor pretty, rich boy isn't getting what he wants.

He continued flicking through the pages rapidly and when he paused again; he had reached my name. He stared at it, interested.

I snapped the book closed over his fingers and took it from his grasp.

'I am transparent about who I am, unlike some. I got you the ledger and almost got my ass busted for it, so now tell me what I need to know,' I said hastily.

'What you need to know and what you want to know are different. You need to know that you cannot speak of this ever, and that you need to forget all about the journal, Albert Kersey and never return here,' he said.

I patiently waited for him to continue.

'Do you know how to access stored code in crystals?' he asked.

This threw me for a loop. How did everyone know about this but me?

'No...but I have begun learning crystal magic,' I responded, leaving out that it was Abigail teaching me.

'Well, I'm only giving you my answers visually, so I hope you learn fast,' he said.

Before I could even begin to ask what he meant, he grabbed my hand and pulled it towards him in the water. I immediately pulled back, and he chortled.

'Fine. I don't trust you either. Let's agree to not make any moves to kill one another for at least the next ten minutes, then?'

I nodded quietly and allowed him to take my hand once again.

'Close your eyes,' he murmured.

I did as he said, feeling tense despite our agreement.

I felt something rough beneath my fingertips, and a comforting, warm feeling spread through me vigorously. Something about the feeling was familiar, yet I couldn't pinpoint how.

'I wear a tiger's eye, similar to your amethyst. Now, hopefully, you're already receiving the energy stored inside?' he asked quietly.

I nodded.

'Feel the energy in your bones, and envision it combining with your own, feel them melt together.'

I imagined his energy as a glowing orange, and saw it melt into my own blue, cool energy. The combination made me feel more powerful than I ever had in my life. I was sure I could part the falls wide enough to allow the entire district through if I wanted to.

'Now, think to yourself about how you want to access my memory. Concentrate really hard on your intention, and I'm going to try my hardest to let down the barriers blocking them to allow one through. It might not work, crystals will only allow access to those you truly want them to, and I don't know if I do,' he muttered under his breath.

I focused all my energy on seeing Cyrus' memories and feeling his emotions. I felt something coming and going, almost as though he was giving them to me and then quickly retreating.

I felt connected to him in a way I never have with another fae, and I had a strong feeling that I needed to see whatever it was he was trying to show me. With this in mind, I used my other hand to guide the water beneath him to hold him up so he could stand, instead of trying to keep afloat in my element.

I suddenly got a wave of emotion hit me. Anger, grief, loss. Nothing dissimilar to how I have felt myself through the years.

Following the emotion, a grainy image played in my mind. I pushed myself harder to see what was being shown to me and it slowly came into focus from Cyrus' point of view.

I glanced at the clock. Tick, tick, tick.

My father paced up and down the entrance hall, my mother crumpled on the floor crying.

'Why, Reginald? Why our son?' she screeched.

'Stop it, Marie. I don't like it either, but you can't refuse if you are chosen! Do you know what they would do to this family?' he shouted. 'We would be crushed, eliminated. Regular families get memory wiped and moved to a new location. They can't do that to us without wiping the entire district also, and as the most powerful district, they can't afford to do that. Besides, we still have our heir. We will just have to make another spare.'

Mother wailed at his grim tone and clutched onto my brother, Cain. He looked bewildered and frightened, and I felt the urge to go to him. I didn't though. Father was watching my every move to judge my reactions and, therefore, my ability to lead.

Tick, tick, tick.

Thud, thud, thud.

The door banged, and everyone froze. They were here.

My father calmly opened the door and gestured to six enforcement officers from The Centre.

They approached my six year old brother, and spoke.

'Come on, son. Let's not make your mother suffer anymore.'

He looked at me, panicked, and I pushed back the tears in my eyes.

He turned and looked towards mother, seeing her hysterical state, and nodded calmly.

He slowly removed himself from her arms, and she screamed painfully.

He strode towards the officer, and his small hands shook vigorously. He tried to hide it by pressing them flat against his sides. Something about the movement awoke something inside of me, and I rushed toward him.

I grabbed him and put him behind me, sheltering him from the horror he was walking into.

'Wait! Just…wait. If it's blood you want, I'm far more powerful and have far more of it. Suggest a trade?' I pleaded with them, and with my father.

The officers looked at my father expectantly, and he sighed.

A second later, I was being held in the air by a snaking dragon made of hardened magma, impenetrable.

Cain screamed and reached out for me before being swept up by an officer. He cried out, and I shouted pleas until my voice was hoarse. They injected him with something purple, and his small, fragile body went limp in their arms. I watched as they took him away, his little arms trailing beneath him, his teddy, wearing the little red scarf he had made for it, still hidden in his pocket from when I had given it to him this morning.

Mother laid on the floor, her chest racking with sobs. I finally gave up trying to burn my way through my father's magic and allowed myself to sob with her.

Father shut the door behind the officers and looked at me, stone faced.

He strode toward me and gestured the dragon away, dropping me to the floor.

I knew what was coming, but I didn't care. Any pain to mask the one I was feeling now would be welcomed.

He struck me across the face and I tasted blood. He kicked my ribs, hurtling me into the wall.

Mother cried even harder.

He grabbed my jaw, and his eyes blazed red.

'You will NOT disobey me. You will NOT behave like a woman when you are the future leader of this district,' he yelled.

He threw me back to the ground and the pain of my bruised face and broken ribs did nothing to ease the pain in my soul.

'Get up, Marie,' he commanded.

Mother jumped up immediately and wiped her tears, still silently sobbing.

'Go and prepare dinner. We are housing the Asturias family to discuss a trade deal,' he said darkly.

She scampered off and cast me one final apologetic look before turning the corner.

Chapter 5

The vision was ripped away from me and I felt like I had been punched in the heart. I looked at Cyrus, expecting to find tears streaming as mine were, but instead found him cold faced and looking awfully like his father had.

'Cyrus…What was that? What happened to your brother?'

'He was taken to The Centre for blood harvesting.'

'Blood harvesting?' I asked, my mind spinning. 'What does that even mean?'

'Prisoners are kept, and farmed of their blood until they die.'

'Why? For what use?' I asked again, feeling rage build up inside me at the prospect.

'The rich who live there consume it. Blood from another element temporarily gifts you that element. If you consume enough, you will have the extra powers permanently. It's a sick fad and they take hundreds of people from the districts every year. If you're chosen, you can't fight. The vision you saw of your parents being attacked? I saw it too. I don't know what happened to them, but I know the officers in the vision are the same ones who came to collect my baby brother,' he said, his stone cold tone unwavering.

'How do you know all this?' I whispered.

'I'm the next leader of the Fire district. My father has been training me since the day I was born and that means being privy to many secrets.'

I barely listened to his answer as I tried to comprehend this. My parents? The blood farm? Had they not chosen to leave me? Were they not traitors at all? Everything seemed to spin in front of me and I felt as though I was getting very warm. My breathing was shallow, and I felt as though I was floating. And then it went dark.

I came around a short time later and found the floating feeling to have been a Cyrus carrying me out of the water. I still felt warmth, and I looked around to find I was still in his arms.

Cyrus seemed to sense I had come around as I suddenly rolled onto the sandy bank with a thud.

'You passed out,' he said matter of factly.

'I guessed.'

I thought back over his suggestion that my parents were taken, and not traitors who deserted their only child.

I didn't allow myself to feel more grief or confusion, and most of all, not hope. I pushed the thoughts deep down.

Either way, they were gone and there was no changing that now.

I thought back over the scene Cyrus had allowed me to see and thought of the young boy. He looked familiar, very familiar.

'Do you know what happened to your brother?' I asked, not wanting to voice my suspicions if I was wrong.

He looked at me quizzically.

'Why do you ask that? What happened to him is obvious. What are you thinking?' he said.

I chewed on my cheek nervously. I had a strong feeling but I couldn't voice it. If I was wrong, it would only hurt him again. I had no particular care for Cyrus, but toying with someone's grief was cruel.

He clearly sensed my hesitation and gripped my leg, which was crossed in front of me.

He said nothing, but looked at me pleadingly.

I sighed and tried to ignore the tingles travelling up my thigh.

'Marcus' new adopted son, he looks….similar to your brother. He looks older, around 12 years old, but his clothes, his hair and eyes…they're all the same. He seemed strained and uncomfortable in the water…so if his water powers are temporary his lungs probably won't adjust to the lack of oxygen properly…' I trailed off as I realised I was voicing far more than I had wanted to.

'It only happened a year ago. It can't be him. He would only be seven years old,' he said, shaking his head.

I thought about this, about to agree, when I remembered what Abigail showed me.

'Abigail!' I said in realisation.

'What?'

'Abigail has been giving her blood for years, and although she's around my age, her hands are covered in wrinkles and her veins are varicose. She explained how giving your blood ages you to an old woman, and her mother died aged only 32 despite being perfectly healthy. Giving blood ages you!' I rattled.

Could it be true? Could he be Cyrus' brother?

He stared at me so hard I thought he could see through me.

'Kaimana, I know we don't trust each other, and I know we have no reason to. This is our third meeting and yet our third attempt at killing each other was today.'

'I have never tried to…' I started.

'But I need you to do yet another thing for me,' he interrupted.

I looked at him suspiciously.

'I need you to try to talk to Alastor. Find out what he knows or remembers of The Centre. He might say something important,' he pleaded.

I bit my lip and tasted blood run into my mouth. It would be easy enough to do, he had study sessions at the library today as Zach pointed out. But was I getting myself into something that was way out of my depth?

No. This was no longer my business. Cyrus was dangerous. He was involved in dark magic, dark business, and with dark people. I didn't need any more darkness in my life.

'Okay,' I found myself saying mechanically. 'I will talk to him. He's studying at the library I work at today. I'll meet you back here tonight and tell you what I hear.'

His face softened ever so slightly, and a tiny smile tugged at his lips.

I didn't return it. *Why had I agreed?*

It was that damn charisma charm. Leo's were already incredibly enticing people, so having an extra load of charm placed upon him made it almost impossible to resist doing as he wanted.

I took the ledger and headed back to the falls, feeling weak and shaken up from today's events. I parted the falls slightly and passed through the first curtain of water.

'Argh!' I heard a voice cry behind me.

I whipped around to see Cyrus pressed behind me, writhing in agony.

He had followed me behind the falls!

Clearly, he was much larger than me, and had taken damage from the cascading water.

'What on earth are you doing?' I cried.

'I can't just sit and wait for you. I need to come with you, but I knew you'd say no,' he explained through gritted teeth, hands rubbing his arms, one of which was already black and blue.

'Are you crazy? I don't have the strength to open them back up again! You can't come into the Water district, Cyrus. That's absurd. You need to share your energy with me to open up the falls wide enough for you,' I demanded, feeling incredulous.

'No. I'm coming with you.'

I let out a cry of exasperation and weighed up my options. I could open the falls to let him back into no-man's land, but then I wouldn't have enough strength to get myself into the district. If I left him here between the falls and the cliff, he would only end up drowning or blowing himself to pieces. I didn't find that I particularly cared if he lived or died, but I didn't want it on my shoulders.

'You won't even be able to breathe,' I pointed out.

He pulled a dagger from his boot, embellished with golden cross guards marking the hilt.

I looked at it, confused. He grabbed my hand and pulled it toward him. With a sharp slice across my palm, blood flowed freely, dripping down my arm and into the water.

'What the hell are you doing?' I snapped, trying to pull my hand from his grip. He held on like a vice, and leaned down to kiss...no, suck the cut on my palm. I soon realised what he was doing.

He was insane. He had actually gone mad. The very thing he was trying to avenge, he was asking me to do. Let alone if we got caught, we'd be killed on sight!

I sent a blast of water at him, knocking him sideways, to release my arm.

He mumbled a few incomprehensible words and then looked at me in surprise.

'Thanks, doll. You can't do anything to hurt me now. We're even,' he laughed.

'Hurt you?' I scowled, looking at the cut across my palm.

He took my hand again and pressed his against mine. I felt warmth, and when he removed his hand, my cut had healed into a scar.

'It was only a few drops, but we need to be quick,' he urged.

'I haven't agreed to anything! You are not coming with me. Enjoy your new stolen power out here and use it to stop yourself from drowning.'

He raised an eyebrow at me and spoke calmly. 'I am. Open the falls, now.'

I groaned in frustration as I yet again found myself wanting to bend to his will.

'How do you do that?' I asked.

'Do what?'

'Make me want to do as you say? My mind knows I want you as far away from me as possible, but my body acts on your demands regardless,' I said.

'Probably all the spells I had put on me as a baby,' he shrugged. 'No good having a leader if the people won't do as he says.'

Great. I scowled at him again, and he returned it fervently.

'Heal yourself,' I demanded. 'We'll be stared at even more than usual.'

I looked at his black and blue shoulder. It had to be broken.

'I can't,' he said. 'I can only heal one injury a day. It's my special ability as the heir, but it's limited,' he shrugged.

I felt a certain surprise that he chose to heal my small cut instead of what looked like his broken shoulder.

'It is broken,' he said, glancing at his shoulder and seemingly reading my thoughts. 'But it's fine. I've had it worse. Open the falls.'

I shook my head disapprovingly and turned to part the falls into the district.

'Stay close to me. It's going to take all my power to open them wide enough for you so I won't be able to hold it for long,' I explained.

I focused on taking control of the falling water and manipulated it to move apart as wide as I could manage. I quickly pushed forwards, feeling Cyrus pressed right up behind me.

When I felt he had also made it through, I let go of control and let my shaking arms drop to my sides.

'You must come from a powerful lineage,' he remarked.

'Why?'

'I make it through my district because I'm exceptionally powerful and born to lead a district,' he explained. 'You make it through and seemingly have nothing special about you. It just doesn't make sense. Plus, you managed to break through my dark magic earlier...strange.'

I rolled my eyes at the way he spoke of me. He and Abigail were similar, both born into privilege and tragedy, and yet lacked the sensitivity toward those of us lower down the ladder. I bet he had never worked a day in his life.

'We need to go down now, so we'll swim quickly. Lucky for you, I live above the shore. Only me and two others do. If I had lived below water like the rest of the district, you'd be dead,' I deadpanned.

'Or you would be, when I drank all your blood,' he said. I ignored his remark, that felt awfully like a threat, and swam downwards, always watching him in the corner of my eye.

We swam toward the city centre, him managing to keep up with me perfectly. He gaped in wonderment at the masses of coral, sea beds and plants. A few straggling sea creatures dotted around the outskirts of the city and he looked amazed. Our towering buildings were covered with sea moss and were clear the whole way round, allowing maximum visibility from the sun shining above. He held his hand in front of him and let it glisten in a ray of sunshine beaming through the aquamarine water.

The constant rainbow of colour had him mesmerised, and I had to grab his elbow several times to keep him moving. Despite the fact that most of the fae had not yet awoken, I knew his dark features and obscure clothing would draw attention to him and put both of us in more jeopardy.

We reached the shallows just as he hit my arm repeatedly and started to turn purple. I grabbed hold of him and swam speedily to the surface. We climbed out and he gasped for air - a sight I was beginning to get used to. I led him up towards my cottage, suddenly self-conscious. He undoubtedly came from some huge mansion like the Asturias'. Probably even more grand, considering Fire was the second most powerful.

I opened my door and ushered him inside before anyone could see us. He stepped through and stopped in the small bedroom I called my own, looking around.

I followed behind him and showed him what there was to show.

'This is the living room, and then the kitchen's through there,'- I pointed through my living room that contained one small sofa, into the kitchen that barely had enough space for two people to stand in - 'and there's the bedroom and bathroom and yeah... that's it...'

'It's very cosy,' he said quietly.

I appreciated that he didn't outright insult me as I had expected, and just continued to talk.

'I have to go to the library, so you stay here. The journals are on my bed and you can make yourself...comfortable,' I said.

I felt like I was leaving a ticking time bomb in my home, but I didn't have a choice.

I quickly got my blue swimwear from the washing and closed myself in the bathroom to change.

'Put the red back on,' he said simply.

I looked at myself in the mirror. I suppose the red really didn't look that bad. Sure, I was conspicuous, but I always was anyway.

I kept the red swimwear on and headed out, ready to leave for the library.

'Don't make a single noise, don't go outside and don't cause trouble. I'll be back in six hours,' I commanded, and with that, I shut the door behind me and dived back beneath the surface.

I had expected him to argue, demand to come with me. He had already taken my blood. Why not this time? My only peace of mind came from the fact that he wouldn't kill me - he needed my blood to breathe here, and he wouldn't do anything too absurd, otherwise I wouldn't let him out of the district.

~

I made it to the library just before opening time and hurried to sign in.

Paula smiled at me warmly, and I returned it wholeheartedly. I wished I could talk to her about my parents, but I couldn't risk implicating her.

Zach immediately bustled over to me.

'Hey babe, glad to see you. What are you up to tonight? I thought we could…'

'Zach, I'm sorry but I'm busy tonight and we aren't back together so I really think we should keep things friendly,' I interrupted him, fed up with his pestering.

I expected him to pout and guilt trip me, but instead he winked.

'Sure thing, Kaia. We are soooo not back together,' he said in an over exaggerated tone and glancing toward Paula.

I groaned and swam away from him.

Moments later, the Asturias children arrived, guards in tow.

'Greetings!' boomed Castor's voice. 'We are here to commence with our studies, and we are so grateful for your hospitality. As thanks, we will be giving you all signed photographs.'

He smiled gleefully, as if this was an extraordinary honour.

I met eyes with Angela across the room and she smiled playfully, and rolled her eyes.

They were escorted to their private area of the library, Alastor smiling at the staff as he went, Castor simply picking at his nails.

For hours, the children flicked through books and occasionally wrote some things down. The guards never left their side, and I saw no opportunity to get close to Alastor.

I busied myself around the place, always keeping a close eye.

The bell rang to indicate someone had entered through the main doors, and I headed over to let them know the library was closed for the day.

'Excuse me, sorry. The library has been reserved for…oh! Hi, Abigail. What are you doing here?' I said, surprised.

'Kaimana! I didn't know you worked here,' she said in a hushed voice.

I nodded sheepishly, and she swam past me.

'I'm looking for a new reading collection. It seems I have read everything there is to read in my house, and I'm starting to get awfully bored,' she explained.

'Okay, no problem. Except the library is actually shut today because…' I tried to say again.

'Oh, nonsense. Castor will be delighted to see me,' she interrupted before swimming off toward Castor and Alastor.

I gulped as I chased after her, awaiting the reprimanding from the enforcement officers, but they simply nodded to her and allowed her to approach the heirs.

'Abigail!' Castor said politely, though I noticed he rolled his eyes as he stood up. 'How are you?'

'Fabulous. Will you introduce me to your brother?' she asked sweetly.

I watched the interaction with interest as an idea began forming in my mind.

'Of course. Alastor, this is Abigail. She's…well, she's a friend.'

'Hello, Abigail,' Alastor smiled.

She nodded to him politely.

'How are you, dear? You must be struggling to adjust in such an unfamiliar environment. How exactly is it that you were orphaned?' she asked.

Alastor's smile faltered, and Castor quickly interjected.

'Now, Abigail. You know what my father says about your directness. Don't barrage the poor lad,' he chuckled.

'My apologies,' she said sincerely to Alastor.

They spoke a little more about general affairs, and then she said her goodbyes and Castor wished her well.

She turned and swam back toward me, smiling.

'So, what do you recommend?' she asked.

'Recommend?'

'Books, dear,' she said exasperatedly.

'Oh, right. Yeah, follow me.'

We swam through various rows of the library and each book I pointed out, she chucked into the basket on her arm without bothering to look at it.

'So how come you've done so much reading?' I asked.

'Not much else to do when you live alone,' she smiled.

'I understand that. I've lived alone for a while too.'

'I dare say you should come and stay with me for a night! It could be fun,' she suggested excitedly.

'Erm…well I can't tonight,' I said, thinking of Cyrus at home.

'Of course not. Sorry. Silly of me really, we've hardly met.'

'No, that's not it,' I said, not wanting to be impolite, though I did secretly agree. 'Why don't you come over tomorrow? We can talk and maybe do another lesson? If you want to.'

'I would love to!' she said eagerly. 'You have my address. Send me a letter with your home address on it and I will come to you.'

I nodded and checked out her books, promising to send a letter straight after work. I watched her leave and smiled to myself. She may have just become my second ever friend.

~

The rest of my shift passed quickly, and a mere 20 minutes before I was due to leave, I began to panic. How could I make contact with Alastor without the guards stopping me or overhearing me?

I began to plot, when he suddenly got up from his seat. I watched him closely and realised he had already been through all the books provided to him, and was swimming toward some shelves to hunt for more. I raced over and organised books on the shelf opposite him.

'Hi,' I said gingerly.

'Oh, hi,' he responded, glancing at the guards.

'Don't worry, I'm not some crazy fan. I just wanted to see how you were settling in,' I probed.

'Oh, yes, fantastic. Thank you,' he smiled.

How was I supposed to get anything real out of him? *Hi Alastor, were you kidnapped and harvested for blood by any chance?* Not likely.

'I see you met Abigail,' I smiled.

'Oh, yes. Do you know her?'

'Yeah, she's a…friend.'

'She seems to be everyone's friend,' he laughed quietly.

'Well, that's the thing with Abigail. She doesn't give you much choice.'

He smiled and continued looking through the books in front of him.

'I was sorry to hear about your parents,' I said softly.

'Thanks. Yeah, they were, erm, great people, or were they not? I'm not sure…' his voice trailed off almost incoherently quiet.

'So, how does the district fare to The Centre?' I asked more lightly.

'The Centre…?' he asked.

'Sorry, the Central Island,' I replied, using the ponced up term the rich families used.

'Oh, well, I'm not too sure… It's beautiful,' he finally settled on, and turned with some books, back to his chair.

I cursed internally. That told me nothing except he was a little confused.

I headed round to where he had been looking and tried to see what books had been removed. He had taken books on the history of the district families.

I was about to give up and head home, when Jazlean King and her Jaz Hands blocked my path out.

'Aww, is Kaia buddying up to the new guy?' she sneered. 'You know, just because both your parents are dead doesn't mean he's going to want to associate with you.' Her group of followers cackled behind her.

'You got me, Jazlean,' I responded, rolling my eyes. She had taunted me mercilessly in school over my parents, but I had grown stronger because of it. Her comments meant nothing to me.

Just as I went to push past her, I noticed something lying on the floor by her feet.

A small, tattered teddy with a red scarf.

This was the pocket teddy the young boy had in Cyrus' vision. This was Cain! It had to be.

'You know, actually, you're soooo right,' I remarked to Jaz, my voice drawling as hers did.

She looked confused, but nodded anyway.

'My parents *are* dead. They were traitors. Maybe they cursed me,' I suggested.

'Probably,' she smirked.

I clutched my necklace in mock horror.

'This crystal holds traitorous magic then…'

I dived toward her, arms outstretched, and as predicted, she jumped backward and screamed.

I swerved to the side and picked up the teddy, smiling to myself.

Jazlean and her Jaz Hands spat out a string of profanities my way, and I chuckled to myself as I went to sign out. Trust her to think traitorism is contagious.

I signed out and briefly noticed that Zach had already signed himself out, which was unusual for him, but paid it no real attention.

Just as I left the library doors, I noticed Angela standing in the corner, her gaze fixated on me. I smiled a little but she didn't return it. Odd.

~

I stopped off to post my address to Abigail as promised, cursing at the cost of six lunas for next day postage, and then arrived back at my home. Pulling myself out of the water and onto land, I realised why Zach was already signed out. He was waiting at my front door.

'Hey babe,' he smiled.

'Zach, what are you doing?' I sighed.

I noticed something moving behind Zach's shoulder and saw my bedroom curtain twitch and realised Cyrus was listening in.

'I thought we could chill tonight, have some dinner...' he said, winding his arms around my waist.

'Zach, I was serious earlier when I said we aren't back together. You know how I feel, and I just want to be friends.'

'Oh. I thought that was for show,' he frowned.

I shook my head and stepped back.

'Why don't we just try again though, Kaia?' he began.

I sighed again and felt myself getting frustrated.

'Zach, I don't want to lose you as a friend…' I started to shut him down.

He lunged forward and grabbed me, kissing roughly. I writhed and tried to pull back, but he gripped me tightly. Just as my arm wound back to slap his cheek, he was suddenly yanked away.

Cyrus had Zach's throat in his grip, and had lifted him into the air. His eyes were still a melting shade of brown, but they blazed with fury.

Despite Zach being a well-trained athlete, his strength had nothing on Cyrus'. He wriggled pointlessly whilst Cyrus kept him suspended with only one hand, his other one outstretched and ready to burn.

'Cyrus!' I shouted, my heart racing wildly.

'You think that's cute? You think you can touch her without her permission?' he roared.

Zach shook his head manically and kept looking back at me, wide eyed.

'Cyrus. Let go,' I said, calmly.

'Keep your filthy hands away from her, or you will *never* use them again,' Cyrus hissed between gritted teeth.

Zach nodded, and Cyrus dropped him to the floor in a heap, shaking in anger.

I dropped down to Zach and offered my hand to him. He looked at Cyrus warily and didn't take it, instead using a plant pot to push himself upright.

'Come here again, and I promise I'll not only take you out, but I'll burn your whole house to the ground, and let your family's screams play like music to my ears,' he spat viciously.

I looked at Cyrus in shock, but his eyes remained fixed menacingly on Zach.

Saying nothing, Zach scampered into the water and took off faster than I had ever seen him swim before.

I stalked towards Cyrus and shoved his shoulder backwards.

'What the HELL was that?' I exclaimed.

He said nothing and just looked at me, anger still tearing through his features.

I was mindful of my neighbours and the scene that had just been caused, so I opened the front door and pointed for him to go inside.

He, surprisingly, complied without complaint and walked straight through to my bedroom.

I followed him in, intending to give him a turn at feeling my anger, but he had stopped dead in the doorway.

I frowned at him in confusion and struggled to read the expression on his face.

He strode towards me, breathing heavily, and stopped mere inches away from my face, and then tipped his head back and looked at the ceiling, expelling a large breath of air. I forced myself not to step backward. He gripped on to the door frame and seemed to be having a hard time collecting himself.

'Why did you do that?' I asked incredulously.

His eyes looked down to meet mine, and I felt a mixture of fear and excitement race through my limbs.

'Because anyone who behaves like that deserves it,' he replied finally.

'Like what? He kissed me. He didn't bloody attack me!'

'Would you just stop?' he snapped. 'I'll leave you then, next time some guy is forcing himself on you.'

'Like you?' I asked quietly.

He whipped his head down to look at me.

'Like when you grabbed me and wouldn't let go? Slicing my hand and forcefully taking my blood? *That* is when I need to defend myself. And I am perfectly capable of defending myself when it is *necessary*.'

He looked at me in shock, and his eyes roamed across my expression wildly. I tried not to show any feeling, for the way I was feeling was nonsensical. Why did I feel hurt? As though we'd had any foundation of trust in the first place? Of course we hadn't. And I should expect no less from the Fire heir than to take what he wants without mercy.

'I did what I had to do. I took no pleasure in handling a woman that way,' he said grimly, his expression dark and unforgiving. 'You know, I thought you were someone with half a brain, unlike your fellow residents. I thought you would actually be useful in helping me find my brother, but clearly not. Every single time, you've been slow on the uptake. The journal, meeting me, your own parents' death, for crying out loud! So, obviously, I was mistaken. Let me out of the district.'

I tried not to feel the hurt that was worming its way into my heart. His words meant nothing to me, he was nothing to me. Cyrus was a man made of monster, and I wished with my entire being that I had never gone to no-man's land to begin with.

But his little brother didn't deserve to be left stranded. Without speaking, I pulled out the teddy and held it up for Cyrus to see.

He looked at it, then at me, and fell to the ground.

Chapter 6

I stared, confused. Cyrus was crumpled on the floor, breathing even heavier than he had been.

I could already feel my icy resolve thawing, and wanted to reassure him, but there was no way I would be offering him comfort after the way he had just acted.

I dropped the teddy in front of him and walked past.

'You can sleep in the living room, we're seeing Abigail tomorrow,' I said coolly, and then shut the bathroom door.

I stared at myself in the mirror, my mind screaming at me so loudly that I should be taking him out of the district. He had his confirmation, now it was nothing to do with me. He was unstable, unpredictable and incredibly unpleasant. I didn't need to involve myself anymore.

But images of the young boy being dragged from his home lifeless, sounds of Cyrus sobbing, and my own pressing questions about my parents kept circling in my brain, and I knew I had to see this through. Whatever 'this' was.

I waited until I heard the sofa creak, and I knew he was out of the bedroom. I went back through and turned all the lights off, crawling into bed.

What felt like hours passed, spent tossing and turning, and unable to sort my own questions out in my head. Why had Cyrus attacked Zach like that? What would I say to Zach? What am I going to say to Paula about all of this? How are we going to do anything about the fact Alastor is actually Cain? Were my parents taken?

And then the one that I was desperately trying to ignore…were my parents even dead?

I got up to make myself some tea after it became evident that I was not going to be sleeping anytime soon, and passed Cyrus, sleeping on the sofa. I noticed the way he was holding his arm with one hand and holding the teddy in the other. Guilt wracked through me as I remembered he still had a broken shoulder.

I went to the kitchen cupboards and began rummaging for some bandages that I could makeshift into a sling, when I felt a presence behind me.

I didn't turn, partially because I knew who it was, and partially because it was so tight for space in here, that if I tried to turn, I would end up rubbing up against him. Which I did *not* want to do, as I reminded myself.

'I didn't think you were awake,' I commented.
'I wasn't.'

His breath tickled the back of my neck and I inhaled the scent of spearmint and smoke, a smell I was now becoming very used to.

'Sorry I woke you up.'

His breath raised goosebumps on the back of my neck and sent shivers cascading down my spine.

I finally gave in and turned around. My face was in level with his chest and I looked up at his face, never truly realising how tall he was until now. He was already looking down at me, and then shifted forward. We were now completely pressed together, and when he spoke, I could feel the vibration of his words echoing throughout my body, and I had to fight not to lose focus.

'What do you have there?' he asked in a low voice, looking at the bandages in my hands.

'For your shoulder,' I said, without moving.

He pulled off his buttoned shirt in one movement and waited expectantly.

I swallowed thickly as I looked at the muscles running throughout his tanned torso. I gently took his arm and folded it over so it was pressed against his chest, and felt the same warmth I was now all too familiar with dancing across my skin and penetrating my veins.

His biceps flexed and I couldn't help but watch appreciatively. He didn't look as wide and robust as the enforcement officers did. He appeared lean and subtly defined...when his clothes were still on.

I tentatively wrapped the bandage around his neck, bringing it underneath his arm tightly, to hold it in place.

It wasn't the best fix, but it was all I had for the time being.

'It's not going to hold for ages, but it'll stay for the night and you can heal yourself tomorrow,' I said.

He nodded and then lifted his other hand up to my face. I kept deathly still. His fingertips traced my jaw, lips, chin, down my neck, and then he dropped his hand to his side.

'I do wonder why our paths crossed,' he murmured so quietly I almost didn't hear.

'It's been a string of unfortunate coincidences,' I said bleakly.

'That's true. However, I do believe that nothing is ever truly a coincidence.'

'Well, there's one thing we agree on then,' I muttered.

'Yes, and they seem to be far and few between. It does create the idea that perhaps this was destined for us all along.'

I stayed silent while his thoughts seemed to be keeping his focus.

'Are you a Pisces?' he asked.

What an odd turn in the conversation.

'Yes,' I answered. 'How did you know?'

'You're pretty impulsive. You act on emotion, not logical thought. You're so quick to be manipulated. How many times have we fought but you've still remained complacent afterwards in order to hear what I had to say? You allowed me into your home despite being completely against the idea. I will say your general intuition about things seems to be right on the money.'

'The same could be said about you, could it not? Yes, I have stayed to listen after we have fought, but so have you. You are the one who entered yourself into my world, having to blindly trust me despite me being barbarous, as you described it,' I said.

'Maybe not as slow on the uptake as I thought. I like you proving me wrong, Green,' he smirked in the darkness.

'Go on then. I know you've made a guess at my sign.'

I thought back to my impression during our first conversation.

'You're a Leo,' I said confidently. 'You're confident, charismatic and you go for what you want, no matter what. But you're self-centred and stubborn. '

'Right on the money,' he whispered, coming closer to me still.

I cleared my throat and turned my head to the side, trying to put some distance between our faces, which were now almost touching.

He caught my chin and turned my head back to face him. 'Don't look away.'

I did as he said and kept my face forward. His eyes, though hard to see in the dark, blazed with something I couldn't pinpoint.

'What do you want?' I asked, fed up with his mind games. We seemed to be in a constant cycle of violence and destruction, to being part of some temporary alliance.

'Many things. I want to be released of my title to the Fire district. I want to save my brother,' he began.

'Oh, is that all?' I remarked.

'Nope. I want to eliminate the districts,' he replied smoothly.

I faltered. Eliminate the districts? Why would he want that? Is that what his plan has been all along, using the ruse of his brother?

'Cyrus…' I whispered, scared to continue down this road of conversation.

'I want to be able to act as I please, within reason. I don't care for the responsibilities I have in Fire. I don't care to go back to my life the way it was. If I manage to save Cain, I would never be able to return, anyway. Plus…I admit I still feel as though you are incredibly dangerous to me. I can see myself failing because of you, but I do feel that I was meant to meet you that day in no-man's land. Coincidence is a myth, and it makes me wonder if there is more in our destiny than just some weak, untrustworthy alliance. All the tension, the chaos, the fighting…I find myself craving it when it's gone,' he professed.

What? How many times had he insulted me? Stripped me of my will? When really he 'wonders' if there is more to us than what we currently were? I could've sworn I heard tiny little alarm bells ringing in the back of my mind. What a shame I love percussion.

'That's a big statement,' I responded simply.

'Don't you feel it?' he asked, brows furrowed.

Admittedly, I did feel something. I felt like he warmed me up inside, like finally sitting beside a fire on a cold, cold day. I didn't realise how much coldness I'd been through until I felt his touch.

He clearly read this on my face and smirked.

Electric energy pulsed between us as the tension of our words amped up. I was sure there was nothing between us more than some sexual chemistry, but that was enough to set my soul ablaze.

He leant in towards me, and I anticipated him to go in for a kiss. Instead, he took his lips to my collarbone, brushing along the contour of my shoulder. I fought not to move my own hands to his shoulders. It was the most comforting yet electrifying thing I had ever felt. His hands wound behind my waist slowly, and I dared not to move. His face was pressed next to mine as he slowly trailed up my neck, and I inhaled the scent of him. Spearmint, leather and…what I could only describe as smoke. I had never smelt it much, only once or twice above land from the Fire district, or the rare occasion when I had real food to attempt cooking.

I leant into the warmth of him and felt my heart slow as pure belonging washed over me. Was he right? Were we meant to have found each other? This sure felt like it.

His mouth and nose brushed my jaw, and I heard him inhale. I wondered what I smelt like. Probably not half as good as he did.

As if reading my thoughts, he spoke softly.

'Lilies, sea salt and jasmine.'

I wondered where he had smelt any of those things before in Fire. I knew I hadn't in Water, bar sea salt. No flowers grew above land, but I had seen pictures of them in books, and they looked appealing at least.

I didn't respond for fear of what I was sure would be my shaky voice.

I finally placed my hands on his chest and felt the energy flowing between us. He pulled back slightly, and I wondered if he was finally going to kiss me, every inch of me now craving it. But he only pulled back and removed his hands from my lower back.

'I can't,' he whispered, shaking his head.

I stayed silent, not knowing why he couldn't, but not asking either.

'Cyrus?'

'Yes?'

'Will you tell me what that magic was this morning? The runes, the cage of heat?' I whispered.

His gaze dropped from mine, and his expression hardened.

'I've been learning dark magic since I was young. Being leader of a district means you have to have a certain edge. Know you can defeat your enemy no matter what.

My father taught me the spells, the defences, but he never taught me how to control it.

I will admit I feel…vulnerable. And whether that be due to the fact that I'm on a mission to save my supposedly dead brother or because I can never trust that you aren't going to kill me at any moment, it puts me on edge.

When you sent that water at me, I reacted without logically thinking that you probably weren't trying to kill me this time.'

I pondered his words for a moment before deciding I believed him.

'You must trust me, though,' I said. 'You've left your district and are completely trapped here without me.'

'Not quite,' he replied, his tone morphing into something much darker than it had been before. 'I could always take your blood and let myself back out. Your blood grants me your power, including to manipulate water. I'm much more powerful than you. I'm sure I could open the falls. I won't though. Not unless you leave me no other choice.'

I stared at him in shock. I had never even considered he could do that. I had been banking on the fact he wouldn't harm me for the sake of mutual destruction.

'Unless I leave you no choice?' I asked in a quiet voice.

'If you attack me, or you stop me from what I'm trying to do, I won't have a choice.'

I said nothing and felt humility creep into my heart as I realised he had played me for a fool. Sweet words and whispered confessions had been enough for me to forget he was one of the most powerful fae in our world, and would always take what he wants before anything else. He was using me to gain access to his brother, and that was all.

He sighed and turned around.

'I'll see you tomorrow, Kaimana.'

I watched as he walked back into my living room, the muscles in his back illuminated slightly beneath the moonlight, and listened as the sofa creaked under his weight.

I allowed my heart to return to its normal pace and finally headed through to go to bed.

As I walked past him, eyes closed and on the sofa, he reached out and grabbed my hand, planting a soft kiss on my knuckles.

Chapter 7

The sun arose the next morning, greeting me after only a short two hours sleep. My body had been far too awake to drift into sleep despite my mind being completely frazzled.

I noticed that yet again my fleeting sleep had been unbothered by nightmares and wondered if it had something to do with Cyrus.

The thought of Cyrus brought back vivid memories of the night before,

His brief kiss had kept me up for hours, wondering what it meant. Was it an apology for his threat? Or was it affection of acceptance? That he knew how things had to be between us?

I dressed immediately and got ready for Abigail's arrival. I had decided Cyrus needed to meet her, maybe coax her into giving more information so we could understand what was happening to his brother. If she was in regular contact with government officials, she must know something…

I busied around making sure everything looked as nice as I could make it, and finally stopped putting off walking into the lounge.

Cyrus was awake, sitting up and healing his shoulder.

'Abigail will be here soon and you need to look the part,' I said, tossing a pair of my fathers old swimwear at him from the small box of belongings I had been given after their death.

He nodded curtly and then proceeded to strip off right in front of me to change.

I gasped and whipped around so that I wasn't looking at him, and I heard him chuckle.

'Oh come now, Kaimana. We both know you want a peek,' he said in a teasing tone.

I rolled my eyes and waited until I heard the zip of the swimwear to turn back around.

He looked…weird. Blue didn't compliment him as well as his usual white shirt and dark trousers, did not favour the deep tones of his skin and hair, but it would have to do. He grimaced at his reflection in the window and shook his head slightly.

We spent the remaining time avoiding each other, and I noticed he hardly met my eye at all, despite reprimanding me for not holding eye contact with him the night before. I had figured he would be this way. Things said in the dark of night, on a highly emotional day and made sensual by the glow of the moonlight, clearly did not apply during the day.

I didn't let that distract me from what we needed to do. Not that I was 100% sure what it was we were trying to do now…

~

'Hey, sweetie!' Abigail smiled as I opened the front door.

'Hi, Abigail. Come in,' I gestured her inside, awaiting the remarks on my home.

'Oh! How…cosy!' she smiled unconvincingly.

I grimaced as I remembered how Cyrus had described it the exact same way.

'Thanks. Before we start, I want you to meet Cyrus,' I said, bringing her through to the living room.

I held my breath as her eyes scoured over him and then narrowed.

'I haven't seen you around before…what's with the hair?' she asked quizzically.

I shot Cyrus a look, and he raised an eyebrow. I had pre-warned him of her…directness and considering Cyrus' temper, I was glad I had.

'I don't go out much. My mother and father were traitors. They escaped the districts and my father came from Fire, hence my features. Obviously, my mother could only give birth during water sign months, so I was born a Scorpio, and brought here when they died,' he replied easily.

I had advised him to enter in some incriminating details to make Abigail trust him as she had me, but I was surprised by how easily the lie flowed from his lips. He even softened his voice to sound more similar to those of a Water resident.

Abigail looked at him suspiciously before finally looking back at me.

'I see why you keep his company. Though do be advised that just because you are low born doesn't mean you need to lower yourself even further,' she said matter of factly, shooting Cyrus a withering look as she spoke. 'Is this why you were occupied last night?'

I saw Cyrus squash a smirk, and a blush crept into my cheeks.

'I see,' she winked before I could answer.

She proceeded to begin showing me how to access stored memories in crystals and develop more control over the power they gave. I listened, but not intently; Cyrus had inadvertently taught me a lot about controlling the magic in crystals already.

'Let's see if you can access a memory,' she suggested. 'Of course, your parents may not have known about crystal magic either, so it may not work.'

I nodded and focused on her voice.

'Harness the energy in your crystal. Now, focus hard on whose memories you want to see. See them in your mind. Remember how you felt around them.'

I focused hard on a somewhat grainy image of my mother in my mind. Long, red hair and pale skin like mine.

'Now, imagine going into their mind, feel how they felt and bring their energy to the surface of the crystal.'

I focused so intently on my mother and combining her energy with mine, that Abigail's voice fell away into the background.

A wavy, blurry image played in my mind's eye.

'Kaimana,' my mother cooed, looking at a small, red haired baby.

She looked up, into my father's face, which was smiling back at her. His blonde hair fell into his eyes and he kept pushing it backwards.

I gasped and opened my eyes.

'What did you see?' Abigail asked excitedly.

I felt unsettled and shaken at what I had managed to do, and for some reason, my eyes fell to Cyrus for reassurance, but he was staring at Abigail.

'My…my parents, I think. I think they were holding me as a baby,' I breathed shakily.

'What did they say?' Abigail pressed.

'Nothing. Well, just my name.'

'Oh. Well, don't worry. You can keep practising and find better memories in there. It's a learning curve, harnessing that much magic to your will,' she replied before looking at Cyrus. 'What about you? What did you see?'

I looked at him in surprise. I had been so focused that I hadn't realised he was playing along also. Of course, he already knew all this and much, much more than even Abigail.

'Nothing,' he shrugged. 'Guess I need more practice.'

She nodded, as if she had expected this.

'That's okay. Some people are just stronger than others.'

'How do you know so much about all this?' Cyrus asked her, and I looked for her reaction.

She seemed guarded, but not outright distrusting.

'My grandfather was a powerful fae. He passed a lot of knowledge down to us,' she responded.

'Who?' Cyrus pressed, and I shot him a warning look.

'Albert Kersey.'

'Oh, right. Your family must have been to The Centre then?' he asked.

She now looked suspicious.

'I haven't personally. Why?' she said.

'Just wondering. I heard Marcus' new son is from The Centre. What do you reckon?' he asked again, and I crossed the room toward him, ready to pinch his arm if he carried on like this.

'I don't think you should be asking questions like that,' Abigail replied, eyes narrowed.

Cyrus suddenly brought flames to life in his hands, and my eyes widened in panic. He sent a circle of scorching heat around Abigail.

She didn't even flinch.

'I knew it,' she laughed.

'Knew what?' I asked.

'I knew he had Fire. He's too dark to have lived here his whole life, regardless of his genetics. I can feel the heat coming off him from here. What now then?' she asked Cyrus.

I was astounded by her perception. She was much smarter than I gave her credit for, and I silently prayed she would upkeep her silence on the subject outside of my house.

'I've noticed a few things about you too,' he replied in an aloof voice.

'Enlighten me.'

'Well, combing through your grandfather's journal, there are several references to his golden haired daughter. The district ledger memorialised notable fae right at the back with images and names. Your mother was silver haired. You knew about Alastor despite the story not being published yet, so you know a lot more than you're letting on,' he stated.

'I'm high up in the district. I hear things before the local news,' she sneered.

'We both know that's not true. Your family was disgraced. You keep up this aura of elite status, but the truth is your money is running out, and the district doesn't care,' he retorted.

Her eyes flicked toward her sleeves, and I noticed they were frayed and tearing.

'Let me guess. A Rayos?' she asked, eyebrows raised.

Cyrus' fire stuttered as she made this guess.

'Don't insult me with an answer,' she continued. 'I could tell the moment you outstretched your arm.'

I turned my gaze back to Cyrus and saw a small dragon symbol branded into the skin of his wrist. How had I missed all this?

Cyrus looked at her for a long moment, and then flicked his wrist upward and the fire engulfed Abigail.

I screamed and went to shoot a torrent of water toward the blaze, but he knocked me sideways with his arm and I fell to the ground.

A guttural shriek sounded amidst the blaze, followed by a hoarse voice calling out.

'I know where your parents are, girl!'

My parents? How did Abigail know where they were? Where they were was dead, wasn't it?

From the floor, I sent a shot of water to knock Cyrus off his feet, and with my other hand, doused the flames that had overtaken Abigail. The fire extinguished, and I hurried through the smoke, about to demand Cyrus to heal her, but all that stood in place of Abigail was a pile of black ash.

The smell I once associated with Cyrus now burned my nose, and I took it as a stark reminder of the threat he posed, and who he really was.

I felt like screaming again, but no sound left my throat and tears pricked at my eyes. Abigail had only come here to help me, and somehow her own perceptions had killed her, and now I would never find out what she meant about my parents.

I channelled my guilt into fury and pinned Cyrus to the ground in a relentless onslaught of water. He tried pointlessly to burn enough to render my water into steam, but couldn't burn faster than I could shoot.

I heard him gurgling and making noises, but at that moment, I didn't care.

He had manipulated me just like he did Abigail, and I would end up the same as her if I didn't stop him.

I intended to wait for him to pass out before dragging his ass back to no-man's land. I didn't care to kill him anymore. He wasn't worth the energy I would exert to do it.

Suddenly, my vision blurred and I was sucked into his mind.

I sat with my father in his study, awaiting the next lesson I was to be given.

'Now Cyrus, today I'm teaching you about shadow people,' my father said sternly.

I nodded solemnly.

'Shadow people come from the dark realm. They aren't fae like you and I.

The dark realm consists of another species, one that feeds off of pain. The more pain they create, the stronger their powers become. It's an uncivilised, treacherous place, and no one who has entered the realm has ever survived.'

I knew better than to interrupt and ask questions, but they burned in my throat with desire to find out more.

'Shadow people can't get through to our world unless a gate is opened. There's a gate in every district, and in The Central island, and only those in power can open it with a very special object which I will show you when you are older.

It's the same vice versa. We cannot enter their world unless the gate is open on both sides. However, their gates remain open always, as they are always hoping to get through and absorb the powers from this world.

They have many abilities and hold powers different from ours. They are able to control a fae's autonomy, render them powerless and then take over the corpses to trap others. I don't know what their true form looks like. No one who has seen one has lived to tell the tale. But one thing you must always remember is that if they have taken over a fae's corpse, their eyes will fade into an almost inconceivable colour, and when they wish to use their powers, the eyes will go black. They absorb everything about the corpse, their memories, their personality and quirks, even their attitudes and preferences.

It is possible to eradicate them, but it takes immense magic to do so. If you ever encounter one, you need to use the dark flames I taught you last year to incinerate them. Otherwise, they'll be too strong.

Unfortunately, for most fae, if you have seen enough to get to this point of recognising what is in front of you, you are most likely as good as dead already. This is why it is so important, Cyrus, that you do not ever open the gate, for anyone. If more than one or two got through, our world would end. We would all live in pain and torment, feeding their power to keep themselves alive.'

The image before me disappeared, and I was thrown into another one before I could recover.

I watched Abigail closely. Something about her felt cold, even to me.

My eyes flitted to Kaimana as she followed Abigail's word and tapped into her crystal.

I studied Abigail again, and noticed that between blinks, her eyes appeared black. Surely not.
She looked at me and I closed my eyes quickly, my heart racing.
Without making it too obvious, I dug my nails into the inside of my palm, hard enough to draw blood.
I watched through half closed eyes as 'Abigail' seemed to be driven mad with hunger. Her eyes were coated black, and she was looking wildly between us.
Shadow person.
Why wasn't she attacking? Or should I say 'it'.
My mind went berserk trying to think of how to save Kaimana. She knew nothing of these people and was trusting. Too trusting. She would hate me, but I had to kill her friend.

I dropped to the floor, my vision returned to me, and found Cyrus sitting in front of me with his hand on his tiger's eye.

I looked up, utterly bewildered, unable to comprehend what he had shown me.

'How did you show me that? We weren't touching,' I asked quietly.

'That's your first question?' he asked, raising an eyebrow.

'Okay, well, I don't know, to be honest. I just knew with all my might I had to show you, as I knew you wouldn't listen to my words, and I felt my crystal connect to yours almost instantly and then…well we both saw it.'

I nodded slowly.

I didn't let myself look at the pile of ash beside me.

'Your lack of reaction tells me you're in shock, but this is serious,' he said, sounding as stern as his father.

'I know that much, Cyrus. I may be slow on the uptake, but I'm not braindead,' I deadpanned back. I didn't feel as though I was in shock.

'No, but you don't understand the level of this. Someone has opened a gate, and the fact this shadow person did not attack us, or anyone else for that matter, is telling me two things. First, Abigail has been killed recently; shadow people won't take over rotting corpses. Second, it was looking for me, which means someone has control over it. It came looking for me, acting exactly like Abigail, and knowing far too much about things that a regular shadow person wouldn't. It's been told to come here. But Kaimana, if it knew to come here to find me, and it knew to kill Abigail, that means someone knows about you. Who you are, what you've done, and that I'm here with you. We need to go.'

Chapter 8

A loud bang on the front door made us both crouch down instantly and look at each other in panic.

Cyrus crept toward the window and peeked around the corner.

'Get down!' I hissed.

He did as I said and dropped below the window. I was about to signal him to prepare to fight, when a voice rang out.

'Just me, chicken! I know you're in there because I can smell your cooking!' Paula called.

I breathed a sigh of relief and stood up. Cyrus shot me a puzzled look, and I ushered him into the bedroom, shutting the door behind him.

I opened the door to Paula, feigning a smile.

'Hi, lovey. I know you're avoiding Zachary, but it's unlike you to miss so much work, so I thought I'd pop by with some bits for you!' she explained.

Before I could deter her, she pushed past me into the house and started faffing in the kitchen.

'Thanks, Paula. You didn't need to come by. Sorry I haven't been over to update you. I'm just feeling pretty under the weather,' I said pitifully.

'Oh, darling, don't worry,' she fussed, putting away various tins of things and glancing around the place. 'Oh dear, what happened here?' she asked, pointing to the pile of ash.

I hurried over and swept what remained of Abigail into my hands and chucked it out the window, pain wracking through my chest with guilt.

'As you said, cooking mishap,' I said weakly.

She tutted and turned to head toward the bedroom door. I hurried ahead and blocked her entry, and she frowned.

'Now then, what is going on with you?' she cried. 'I have blankets for you!'

She held up two knitted blankets and my heart warmed, touched by her thoughtfulness, as always.

'I just…I don't…' I stuttered.

'Ah. Say no more, duck. Zachary came in rambling about some lad that had stolen you from him, but I assumed it was his usual delusional drivel. Clearly not, though,' she winked. 'I'll leave these out here then and leave you to it.'

'Thanks, Paula,' I said gratefully, feeling unable to muster up another smile.

'Nonsense. I hope you feel better soon, my darling.'

I pulled her into a hug and let myself feel safe for a moment.

'Oh, sweetheart. You must be feeling unwell! Go and rest now,' she commanded, feeling my forehead.

She knew I wasn't a hugger, I wasn't even a toucher. Not with most people, anyway.

I watched as she headed back into the water and my heart twanged as I wondered if this would be the last time I would see her for a long while. She was the mother I never had and my best friend in one, and I hated that I couldn't tell her what was going on. But I would rather feel the crippling isolation that I felt in that moment than do anything to risk incriminating her into the awful mess I had gotten myself into or put her in harm's way.

I blew out a long breath and headed back to Cyrus.

I found him sitting on my bed, frantically flipping through the parchment with my scrawlings on and the intact half of the journal.

I watched him without really seeing him, my mind distant, hanging on thoughts about my mother and father.

'Cyrus, what do you think she - it - meant about my parents?' I asked, trying not to allow any hope into my heart.

He sighed and looked toward me.

'Honestly? I think it was a manipulation tactic to stay alive,' he replied, continuing to look through the papers.

I thought over this, and although he was most likely right that that thing was only trying to save its own life, I couldn't help but wonder if they had been trapped somewhere all these years.

'What are you looking for?' I eventually asked, sure I
would be able to recite whichever entry he was seeking.
'What? Oh. No, nothing, I just wanted some clues on
location. Who was that that came in just now?'
I hesitated before responding. That felt personal, more so
than even the vision of my parents. Paula was mine, and I
didn't want her to be associated with any of the chaos we
were facing.
'Paula. She's…well she's my boss,' I said eventually.
'Working relationships are different here,' he remarked.
I gave a noncommittal nod and sat on the bed next to
him, feeling like the weight of today's events were
catching up to me.

We were as good as dead, and usually, I wouldn't have
cared all that much but I had grown to care about the fate
of the little boy I met in the library, and had already let
myself feel too much hope toward my parents' fate.

'So, what's next?' I asked, unable to mask the sadness in
my voice.
His hand stretched out, as though to brush my cheek, but
he seemed to catch himself, and dropped it back to his
side.
'You do nothing, Kaimana,' he instructed. 'You've been
far too exposed already, and I can finish this journey on
my own.'
'Are you mad? I'm as good as dead just sitting here
waiting! They know where I live. I sent a damn letter with

my address on it! Whatever your next move is, it's mine too,' I said determinedly.

He shook his head.

'No,' he said firmly. 'I agree you need to relocate, but you can do that in the district, rip your name from the ledger - which you need to return by the way - so that it will take them longer to find you. Then, once you are relocated, change your appearance. Likelihood is, the shadow person was reporting memories straight to the magic source which can be obtained by the controller. In this case, the controller is whoever opened the gate, and the magic source would most likely have been a fragment of crystal.'

'I can't sit here not knowing the truth about my parents. If the shadow people don't kill me, then that will. You should know what that feels like,' I reminded him in a low voice.

He let out a groan of frustration and looked at me, eyes blazing.

'I hope you realise that I can't protect you. I will prioritise my brother. Always,' he said, staring at me hard as though this was supposed to change my mind.

'I don't need your protection.'

He rolled his eyes and continued flicking through the papers. I watched him curiously. I had always assumed Cyrus was a typical man of power. Egotistical, stand-offish and just a pretty face with no real thoughts behind it, but I was certainly wrong about one of those things. Cyrus was very smart. He picked up on so many small details and figured out what they meant before I was aware anything was even happening. Even now, he was taking note of every number listed in any entry throughout the entire journal and I tried to see the relevance, but eventually had to ask.

'What do those mean?'

He ignored me and continued writing them down. Eventually, he finished and looked at the long line of numbers in front of him.

'Fire…' he whispered.

I started to feel frustrated. He was proving himself right about me being slower than him, but I couldn't for the life of me figure out what he was talking about.

'These numbers give us coordinates. I knew long ago that in my half was the second set of coordinates, but at the time I didn't understand the relevance. Now, looking at it all together, it makes perfect sense,' he said, seeming to be talking to himself more than me.

'I don't know if this is some power trip, but I'm still in the dark,' I responded in exasperation.

'Don't you see it? These coordinates are telling us which entrance we need to use to The Centre. There's a crossing in every district, and I had assumed we would go from here, but these coordinates are saying the Fire district. If it's being specified, then it means it's important,' he explained.

The Fire district? My heart thrummed as the realisation set in. I was going to have to enter his world, travel through god knows what conditions, and finally breach The Centre.

The Centre that supposedly was guarded by monsters, hundreds of guards and held thousands of multi element fae.

Great.

~

We spent the rest of the day trying to form a plan, and arguing incessantly over it.

'You are a control freak!' he yelled, after three hours of bickering over what our next steps were.

'Maybe so, but I'm right!'

'You aren't. If we leave now, there'll be too many people still patrolling and looking for me. We need to lie low for a couple of days and wait for the buzz to die down,' he argued.

'No. The more time that the Fire heir is missing, the more chaos it's going to create. Do you really think they're just going to stop looking for you? Besides, what about the shadow people? They know where I live!' I cried.

He shook his head in frustration.

'You don't understand how things work -'

'Don't patronise me,' I snapped.

'But you don't!' he shouted again. 'You think you know things, but you don't. They won't risk releasing more shadow people to look for me. They most likely are still waiting on that one to go back and report to whoever it is that released it in the first place. And as for Fire, well once people are missing 72 hours they are assumed dead, and searches will be called off.'

'Right. So let's get a move on while we're a few steps ahead! Whoever opened the gate to the dark realm still doesn't know you killed their shadow soldier, which means we have the upperhand. As soon as they realise it's not coming back, they'll release more. And as for Fire, that may be the procedure for a normal resident, but do you really believe your father will give up trying to find you when he has no other heir? Your brother is supposed to be dead!' I yelled.

Cyrus flinched at my words, and I realised I had spoken out of line.

'If we do things your way, will you finally shut up? Your constant need to voice your every inner thought is irritating,' he snapped angrily.

I tried to remain calm, as I knew it was my own words that had angered him, but he turned into such an ass when things weren't exactly how he wanted them, and it was beginning to grate on my nerves.

'Screw you! We will do things my way and you will apologise when we survive!' I said, surprising even myself with the authority in my tone.

He rolled his eyes and stalked into the living room, flinging himself down on the sofa.

I felt anger bubbling up inside me. Did he not realise this wasn't just about him now? I had to find out if my parents could be alive, and I wouldn't be able to do that from the Water district.

I knew leaving was basically signing my own death warrant, but I felt like I would rather die trying to find out the truth than sit here for the rest of my days, plagued with guilt and obsession.

I began packing a small bag of essentials and tried to calm my nerves for what was coming next.

'You aren't taking that,' Cyrus said, interrupting my packing.

'What?' I asked incredulously. 'You don't think we need food, water, medicine?'

'Of course I do. But we don't know what of yours has had a trace put upon it. We take ourselves and that is all.'

I sighed and chucked my bag back on the bed.

I guess I'm not taking a bag then, I thought.

We sat quietly as we waited for the right time to leave, and I felt trepidation about my next actions.

I was leaving the Water district, forever. I would never be able to return again, not as myself anyway. They would be looking for me as a fugitive.

And I was doing it all with a man who would trade my life for his in a heartbeat.

Chapter 9

As the sky began to lighten from the all consuming black, to a soft grey, I knew it would soon be time to leave. I headed to my bedroom, ready to change into fresh clothes.

I pulled out another red swimsuit automatically, before realising I had only kept it on at Cyrus' request. I threw it back in the pile and pulled out a blue one. I was fed up with controlling all my actions to suit the will of Cyrus. Maybe his charisma wasn't so strong after all.

We waited for the sun's first rays to rise, and then reluctantly giving Cyrus some more blood, we set off to the district border.

I felt adrenaline, excitement and fear all combine into one emotion, and I didn't know whether to laugh or scream, but either way, I had to go.

We went through my weak spot into no-man's land and got ready to head deep down to where Cyrus had described the passage.

'I only took enough blood to reach the falls, so from here on out I'll be holding my breath as normal - just before you go frolicking off,' Cyrus grumbled.

'Okay, Cy,' I said, using sarcasm to mask my utter terror.

He growled and then dived below the surface and I followed.

A large, unnatural looking rock was embedded in the muddy bank, and giving me a nod to move backwards, Cyrus blasted blazing heat at it.

I watched as the flames left his hands and were immediately extinguished by the water, and a bubbling, boiling stream directly hit the surface. He exerted so much power into it that I could feel the water around me heating despite being 15ft away from him.

After only a few moments, the rock disintegrated, and the rush of the current swept Cyrus beyond it, into a dark passage.

Being a water sign, I didn't even feel the pull of the current, let alone be swept away, but I followed behind him nonetheless.

My heart thrummed as I swam inside, and the water quickly shallowed as the tunnel inclined.

I reached a point where I could begin walking, and strained my eyes in the darkness to find Cyrus.

Suddenly, a mere two inches from my face, a hand emblazoned with flames appeared, and I startled backward. Cyrus grinned at me through them and gestured to me to follow him upwards.

I looked around the tunnel, now illuminated by Cyrus, and noticed as we travelled further upward, the ground became more and more adorned with shards of rusted metal. I became eager to see what the district looked like above land, wondering how it would compare to Water. Cyrus always seemed fascinated by our wildlife, corals and even the brief glimpse of buildings he had seen had caught his attention during our swim.

We soon reached another large rocky surface directly above us, and Cyrus braced himself.

'Move seriously downwards,' he warned. 'This will be hot. To you, anyway.'

I rolled my eyes and headed further down the tunnel, stopping at what I thought was a safe distance.

'Go ahead,' I called up to him.

A roar of fire emanated from his entire body, pummeling the rock and crumbling it like it was nothing.

I watched amazed at this display of power and saw the beauty in his element. The red and orange tones reflected off of his golden skin in beautiful harmony, and he looked like a phoenix reborn.

I was so lost in the majestic display, that I hadn't realised the flames were bouncing back toward me.

I cried out as my entire arm was swallowed by searing heat, and quickly shot water from my palms in an effort to put out the flames.

Cyrus immediately stopped the blaze and shot towards me.

'I told you to stand back!' he reprimanded.

'I did,' I said through gritted teeth. 'But I didn't realise how far I had to go.'

He pressed his smooth palms against my skin and I felt instant relief. Warmth spread through me and despite my pain being from heat, I welcomed it into my skin.

'Your healing power is exceptional,' I breathed, feeling less and less pain.

He furrowed his eyebrows, a look I was becoming accustomed to, and removed his palms.

'I wasn't healing yet,' he said, confused.

I realised this was true as the second his hands left my arm the burns in my flesh reacted angrily.

I yelped again, and he quickly put his hands back on me, a white glow gently illuminating the places he touched.

I watched in fascination as the blisters healed over, and the redness faded back to my usual pale colour.

I couldn't help but feel embarrassed at my reaction to his touch and hoped he hadn't read too much into it.

He finally stopped once my arm was blemish free and looked at me, a perplexed look still across his features.

I cleared my throat and looked past him.

'Does that thing have a timer?' I pointed toward the open gap, which now provided us an exit out of the tunnel.

He looked behind him at where the rock had been.

'Yes. Let's go.'

I headed up toward it and watched as he pulled himself out of the hole and pursed my lips as I realised I would need to do the same. I had the upper body strength of an anemone.

I followed him up, and attempted to do as he had done, and failed miserably to lift myself above the surface. An arm reached down toward me, and I gripped it reluctantly, not liking that yet again I was in need of his help.

I tried to help Cyrus as much as I could, attempting to push up with my free hand, but I knew he was doing most of the work. He pulled me above ground and set me aside from the hole, and before I could turn to thank him, or even appreciate the way his muscles flexed as he did so, my attention was fully grabbed by the environment around me.

We were on a rocky, rough ground, with no plants or any form of life in sight. There were jagged rocks that fractured off into different directions, hundreds of pathways of different heights spreading outward. In between each path of black stone, red hot lava moved slowly along the floor, occasionally spitting out onto the surface beside it.

Scattered all over the floor were pieces and piles of metal, some melted into the ground, and some sharp and sticking outright.

It looked like a wasteland, and I didn't see how life had even managed to evolve here.

'Come on,' called Cyrus. 'We can't hang around.'

Cyrus couldn't afford to be seen, and there weren't many places to take cover. The closest thing to trees were dead trunks scattered across the barren land, exuding wiry looking branches.

He jogged across the land, and I followed behind him, my eyes never resting from the constant scanning of my surroundings. Deep voices carried across to me, and I whipped my head around to see where they had come from.

Far off in the distance, some stone building was towering above the surface, with several men gathered outside. The building was huge. Jagged towers stood up in every corner, making it look like a fairytale castle. A very dark fairytale.

'Is that where you live?' I whispered breathily to Cyrus, observing the wrought iron gates opening and closing.

'That thing?' he chuckled. 'No. That's the district hall.'

I continued to scamper behind him and hid my shock at his blatant disregard to that monstrosity of a building. He must have thought the Water district was laughable.

We eventually reached a large cliff face, and he ducked down low, crawling into a small entrance heading into the cliff.

I dropped down and followed him, wincing as my knees hit the uneven surface. I had been dodging splashes of lava, sharp metal debris and crumbling rocks the entire journey.

When I emerged on the other side, I found myself inside a small, glistening cave.

I looked around in awe. It was like the entirety of the district's beauty had been compressed into one place, leaving the rest of the land wasted and forgotten, and adorning this cave with every scrap of wonderment that had existed.

Crystals of every colour lined the walls, glittering in the reflection of the bright silver metal that embedded the cave.

'We can stay here. As far as I'm aware, I'm the only one who knows about this place. Anyone else who knew would have destroyed it for its gems at first sight,' Cyrus said, settling himself down on the floor.

'Are these all real crystals?' I asked.

'Can't you feel it?'

I closed my eyes and felt around me, and sure enough, thousands of streams of energy criss crossed over one another, like a winding path of train tracks towards me.

I tapped into the magic in my own crystal and found that it felt amplified somehow. I felt as though I could use the magic inside it to bring the entire cliff face down to the ground with one movement.

I opened my eyes and looked at Cyrus, feeling a warmth towards him for bringing me here, despite the fact it was his only option.

He had laid on his side, and turned away from me, leaving me with my thoughts.

I anxiously chewed my cheek as I thought about what we were doing.

Our plan had been to enter The Centre using the route from Fire. Cyrus had worked out that the journal was instructing us to leave from Fire, but I wasn't so sure.

It seemed unnecessarily risky to travel to the place where he was being hunted.

And we did now know that hunted was the correct term. Once we reached The Centre, we planned to stay on the beaches that line the outskirts of The Centre.

The actual part we needed to reach would be much harder to access. Towering defences encircled it, and guards at every entry point checked your identity before allowing you in. We were unsure how we were actually going to get inside, but Cyrus seemed positive that the answer was held at the coordinates he had found.

I eventually laid down beside him, for the fact of there being no other space on the rocky floor, and I winced again as the sharpness of the surface jabbed into my spine.

I kept tossing and turning, my stomach growling angrily in hunger and the floor feeling as though it was heating up, getting hotter every second.

'Would you just rest?' snapped Cyrus. 'We have a long way to travel tomorrow and the sun is already setting. I certainly won't be carrying you if you fall from exhaustion. You can stay there and I'll go myself and see you again when you are imprisoned alongside our families.'

He had barely spoken all day, his demeanour entirely changing when we entered Fire.

He was usually egotistical, arrogant and an all around asshole, but now he seemed…darker. As though a shadow had crept over him and rooted itself in anything that had been redeemable about him.

'The floor is burning, and getting hotter by the second,' I said, keeping my voice level. 'You didn't tell me I needed to bring something to lay on.'

'I can't feel it, can I? How would I know you need to protect yourself from the bloody floor as well? Common sense would indicate you should wear something a bit more covering in the Fire district though,' he sneered.

I growled in frustration, and sat up, keeping all bare skin off of the ground. We were in for a long night.

Chapter 10

Hours passed and my head lulled against the crystals, the only relief from the ever growing heat.

I shifted position for the millionth time, and Cyrus had finally had enough.

'The district is obviously built to keep any non elements out by heating the surface, just the same as yours is flooded by water entirely. Neither of us are going to get any sleep if you don't stop moving around,' he said.

I began to protest, but my arguments were quickly cut short by him slicing his own palm open and holding out a bloody hand toward me.

'Take it,' he commanded.

I shook my head. I was not consuming a fae's blood.

'Take it, or we are both going to die of exhaustion out there. And if you fall, you will get skinned alive by the spitting lava, so hurry up.'

I looked at the blood beginning to drip down his arm.

My stomach turned, and I held back the vomit making its way up my throat.

Closing my eyes and internally squealing, I pushed his hand to my mouth.

'Now drink a fair lot. It may as well last you to travel through the district. Drink it and then say 'potentia transmissio',' Cyrus instructed.

The warm flow of his blood reached my tongue, and I fought not to recoil. It tasted the way smoke smelt. There was no other way to describe it.

I swallowed it down and muttered the words he had told me, and felt a growing heat spread through me, before disappearing entirely.

I took a fair few more gulps and opened my eyes to see Cyrus' usual olive tone had become ashen, and I let go of his hand.

'Are you okay?' I asked, wiping my hand across my mouth.

'Sure,' he muttered.

I paid no attention to his tone and instead focused on the whir of magic I felt travelling through me. I didn't know if it was heightened because of how powerful Cyrus was, or if this was just the extent of the fire element.

I felt no heat, no cold, and I felt strangely as though I was going to expel flames at any moment.

'Fire is an explosive element. Often uncontrollable. Young children are taught how to control their fire before they're taught how to read, so please bear that in mind,' Cyrus implored.

I nodded, feeling giddy on power, and he then turned around to finally rest.

I did not. I sat up for hours more, listening to the soft breath coming from him, and waiting until I knew he was asleep.

My mind was fixed on Paula, hell, even Zach. The only people who had ever shown me kindness and love, I would never see again as myself. I felt tremendous guilt over not saying my goodbyes to Paula, but selfishly, I knew it would hurt too much. I didn't even want her to know I was leaving. She needed to be as clueless as anyone else in case she was questioned.

I thought back to the countless nights I had spent with her in the library growing up, protecting me from my foster families. She had tried to volunteer to foster me many times over the years, but was always declined as she earnt a measly amount of lunas for running the library. Tears silently streaked down my cheeks as I prayed I would survive just to see her again.

~

A few hours passed, and my mind was still wide awake. I quietly crept outside and restrained myself to just shooting out one torrent of fire. I needed to expel some energy, and if I was being honest with myself, I also just wanted to see how powerful it was.

I held out my hands and used them as I would when wielding water, expecting to instead see a wave of flames. However, what danced in front of me was an entwinement of cool blue water and red hot fire, spiralling around one another. I gasped in awe.

Two polar opposites, built to eliminate the other, and yet they managed to work together in complete harmony to create something so beautiful.

Lost in the magic of the display coming from my palms, I was not being aware of my surroundings in the slightest. My first inkling that something was approaching me was a dark shiver that ran down my spine. I quickly withdrew the magic and extinguished the flames to only cover my hand, allowing me to see my surroundings.

Darkness and deadened nature was all I could see, but the goosebumps on my arms had not yet gone, and I was beginning to hear a faint creaking noise.

I peered harder, willing the flames to burn brighter.

A 7ft tall, lizard looking monster, made entirely of metal was staring back at me. Its red eyes burned bright, and its long claws dug into the ground. I began to slowly back away, wanting to get to Cyrus, but the minute I moved, a rattling noise came from it, and it pounced toward me, screeching.

I let out a scream and ran for my life. A quick glance behind me told me that it was gaining on me far quicker than I was running, a spiky tongue made of jagged metal shards hanging from its mouth.

I wheeled around and blasted the fire and water combination at its face, causing it to slow.

'What are you doing?!' shrieked Cyrus. 'Don't use water!'

I immediately stopped the blast of water and instead focused on the fire.

I saw Cyrus was running towards me from the cave, blasting flames at the metal monster in front of me.

My distraction cost me, and it managed to take another leap in my direction, its tongue raking up my leg.

I cried out in agony and it towered over me hungrily. Its red eyes drew closer to my face, and it outright ignored the barrage from Cyrus. It opened its jaw wide, and I braced against the razor sharp teeth that were beginning to close over my head.

Cyrus finally reached me, and he threw himself into the side of the monster, knocking it off of my head.

I jumped up and stumbled backwards.

Cyrus let out a cry and the flames he was firing out of his palms suddenly came from every inch of his body and darkened from orange to a deep red.

I watched curiously as the monster wailed and slowly withered down into a pool of melted metal on the rocky floor.

My panting breath slowly reduced to a normal rate, and I assessed the damage to my leg.

Streaking from my ankle to my calf were lacerations so wide and deep I was sure my bone was right below them. Blood poured from them and I groaned as I sat on the ground.

My vision began to spin and as the adrenaline left my body, the pain of the wounds set in.

Without saying a word, Cyrus scooped me up into his arms and began walking back toward the cave. I took comfort in his arms for a moment and found the pain was slightly lessened. Perhaps it was walking on it that had been the problem.

We reached the cave, and he set me down gently on the floor.

'Can you heal me?' I asked.

'No.'

'What?'

'I already healed you this morning, remember? In the tunnel? I can't heal again until sunrise, which is in about two hours,' he reminded me in a harsh tone.

I groaned again and stopped myself from looking at the cuts. It would only make me queasy.

'What was that thing?' I asked, now panting from exertion to remain still.

'A Metallum. They are horrible creatures who devour fae and melt the bodies in their stomachs, which then adds to their frame. That one out there was probably mid-sized so you're lucky. What the hell were you doing out there?'

I shifted uncomfortably, though not from the pain.

'I heard it out there,' I lied. 'So I went out to see what or who was approaching and *someone* didn't warn me that it could be some metal monster.'

'Why would you go out on your own? That's stupid,' he said bluntly.

'Yeah, it was, considering it was a giant lizard, but if I had known that I obviously wouldn't have done,' I replied, rolling my eyes.

I would never admit that I had been eager to try out his power.

He shook his head disapprovingly.

'How many times do I have to see you hurt before you stop putting yourself in harm's way?' he asked.

'Funny. I don't seem to be in harm's way when I'm not around you,' I snapped back.

'I'm sorry.'

His apology threw me for a loop. Why was he apologising to me?

I said nothing, and just frowned at him instead.

'I meant what I said the other night,' he said, shifting closer to me. 'I am drawn to you and I do feel as though we were put together for a reason. I'm hesitant to allow you to be in harm's way because I need to see why the gods chose us.'

'Why?' I asked, wary of his words.

'I know it doesn't make sense. All we do is fight. Physically, verbally. God, sometimes I even think you're attacking my thoughts. And yet, there has to be a reason. Something we're missing.'

He leant in even closer, his breath tickling my lips, his hands snaking up my arms, causing a shudder to ripple my spine.

My heart raced at a supernatural pace, and I waited for him to lean in and kiss me. Finally.

He was right, of course. There was an unspeakable tension between us that seemed to creep through all of the fighting, arguing, and distrust. I didn't think I wanted him, but I certainly knew I wanted to find out.

He sighed and drew back, seemingly disappointed with something.

Frustration overtook me as yet again, he had made these comments that played like music in my ears. I fell fool to them time and time again, despite him only providing me with reasons why I shouldn't. Plus, he still wouldn't kiss me. It was like he was testing himself, trying to see if he felt anything that was worth his while.

'Why do you do that?' I asked, irritated.

'What?'

'You say all these things, you get all close and then you just…stop. You just pull back and return to being an asshole. If you really felt like that, you wouldn't be so resigned,' I said.

'I don't come any closer, not for the fact that my wonders are untrue, but because I can't.'

'You can't. That's all I ever hear from you. Is there a reason why? Because all I can assume is that you can't, because you know your actions will give away the lie in your words! I refuse to be manipulated by you,' I said.

I suppressed the feelings of hurt that were flooding in and reminded myself he was only doing this to ensure I would help him. His allusions to something 'more' were simply vague promises, enticing me to trust in him.

Wait and see how he acts tomorrow. He'll be a total asshole again. He only cares when it's convenient for him to have you on his team, I reminded myself.

He stayed quiet.

Silently, he turned and laid his head on the ground.

Whether he slept or not, I don't know, but I know that I did not.

〜

I waited anxiously for the first few rays of light to reach the cave, before kicking Cyrus with my good leg and wincing as I did so.

He turned to me, his eyes bloodshot and dark, and without me needing to confirm what I wanted, placed his healing hands on me.

I released a sigh of relief as the glowing light sealed up the gaping hole stretching down my calf, and the incessant throbbing finally ceased.

I watched outside as the sun did nothing to enhance the beauty in the district, not the way it had in Water. Back home, the morning sun penetrated all the way down to the ocean floor, reflected by our largely glass buildings. Plants of every colour imaginable became enhanced beneath the soft glow, and the aquamarine colour of the water seemed to glitter. In Fire, however, the morning light only illuminated the emptiness of the district. For a district forged in fire, it was a cold place to be.

I looked down as Cyrus removed his hands from my leg and saw my wounds fully healed.

'Thank you,' I breathed.

He grunted in response.

'We need to get moving before everyone wakes up. I'm all tapped out of healing already, so for the love of Elorial, contain the stupidity today,' he said.

Knew it.

In actual fact, I knew I shouldn't argue. He was right, I had been reckless. But I did anyway.

'I'll contain my stupidity when you stop inciting it. You're not an innocent party in everything bad that's happened. nine times out of ten, you're the cause!'

He rolled his eyes but otherwise ignored me, and stalked out of the cave, setting off towards the way we had come from the night before.

I tutted at his lack of reaction, and then immediately cursed myself for trying to create an argument. A small, tiny voice in the back of my head was asking if I secretly loved the tension between us that was caused by conflict. It sent adrenaline rushing through me and I felt passionate, fiery and…alive.

Was that not similar to something he had once said himself?

But I dismissed the thought as quickly as it had formed. I hated conflict. I was a Pisces.

Chapter 11

Just as my legs were sure to give way from exhaustion,
annoyingly as Cyrus had predicted, we reached Spyrock
Valley.

The heart of the district.

Skyscraping black buildings towered ominously above us,
and a deathly silence echoed between the rocky chasms.

A small bustle of fae were walking robotically up and
down the pathways, barely speaking to one another as
they passed.

I watched as a group of men, none as finely dressed as
Cyrus, all piled inside of a large container that sat on
wheels, and they were taken away inside a cave.

Several children in matching grey shirts and trousers also
formed a line, slowly moving one by one into a building I
could only assume was a school. There was no
playground, no paintings of rainbows or anything similar.

Only a dark, storied building, with a few measly windows dotted around.

Cyrus pulled my arm aggressively as I stood completely still, taking in the scenery.

'We need to sneak into my estate,' he said in a low voice.

'Your *estate*?' I whispered incredulously.

First of all, he had an estate?! Second of all, wasn't that exactly where we would get caught?

'We need a key to unlock the gate to The Centre, and you need new clothes.' He cast a disapproving look at my blue swimwear, shredded, burnt, and tattered from our journey.

I grumbled quietly and allowed him to pull me toward an iron gate, easily double the size of the Water district hall alone. He pressed his tiger's eye crystal into a small reader, and the gates mechanically opened.

'Everyone should be asleep,' he whispered.

'And if they're not?'

'Well then, we better be quick.'

My heart pumped menacingly, and my body buzzed with danger.

We approached a mansion. Though mansion was an unjust description of the extravagant, and completely excessive size of the house in front of me.

He opened up a second set of iron doors, bolted across the center, and stepped inside.

I knew we needed to be quiet, but I could not contain my gasp.

The inside of his home was made almost entirely of ruby and gold, or so it seemed. The walls were red, with gold trimmings, the same as almost every structure I could see. The doors, the huge winding staircase, even the furniture. He shot me a sharp look to hush and continued dragging me down a hall to the right of the marvellous staircase. Portraits lined the wall, and I tried to catch the names as we flew past. I finally found the one I was looking for.

A younger looking boy, shirtless, chiselled with muscle, wielding a dragon made entirely of flames, staring directly at me.

Cyrusall Reginald Rayos II

'Cyrusall?' I giggled, in spite of myself.

'Shut up.'

I cackled quietly, and he looked at me even more sternly than before and I bit my lip, smiling. All of this grandeur and they chose names like that for their children.

There was an empty gap where the next portrait should have been. Light markings on the wall indicating an image of a person who once stood there, now no more.

Even Cyrus paused briefly at the sight.

'I didn't know they had taken it down,' he said quietly.

I thought of Cain, and how he would have looked in his portrait. I imagined him smiling, holding his teddy, and felt a steely resolve to bring him home.

We continued moving down the never ending corridors until we finally reached an entirely golden door.

Cyrus let go of me, and slowly turned the knob, peeking his head around. He ushered me inside, affirming it was empty, and I realised we were in his bedroom.

A huge, four poster bed sat in the centre of the room, overlooking a wall made only of windows, the only resemblance to Water.

Other than this, and a large, dark walnut wardrobe on the left side of the room, it was empty. He headed over to the wardrobe and pulled out a selection of dresses, chucking them on the bed.

'Pick one and change,' he ordered.

I raised my eyebrow at the offerings.

They were all ridiculous, frilly, round skirt dresses.

'I'm not wearing any of those. Where did you even get them from?' I said.

'You are,' he growled, ignoring my question. 'Pick one, or I will pick one for you and undress you myself.'

I considered this for a moment and decided I would not give in to another one of his blackmails.

'No.'

He strode to the bed, and rummaged through the pile, finally settling on what was agreeably the lesser evil of them all.

A pale, sage green dress. Minimal frills, and a straight falling skirt as opposed to the balloons on the rest of them. It had a white panel in the front and was hemmed with gold.

'Cyrus, I cannot wear that,' I protested. One stitch on that dress was worth more than my entire home and possessions.

He didn't bother to argue with me, instead just walking behind me and unzipping my swimsuit.

I gasped and whirled around, ready to strike him across the cheek, when I realised his eyes were firmly closed, and he was holding out the dress for me to put on.

I sighed and bent to his will yet again, pulling off the remainder of my district clothing.

I took the dress from him, and stepped into it gingerly, pulling the sleeves over my arms and as I did so, I couldn't help but marvel at the feeling of luxury, and felt surprised to find it fit like a glove. I wondered why he even had all these and why he had disregarded my question. It's not as if they lacked the space for his mother's things elsewhere.

'You can open them,' I said softly.

He did just that and stared at me for a few moments before I coughed and turned around.

'Lace me up?'

He nodded and began doing up the strings of the corset that lined the dress, pulling them gently to tie together. All curiosity about whose dress I was wearing fell from my mind as his fingertips electrified everywhere they touched, trailing up my spine as the dress became whole. He held onto my shoulders, and turned me round to face him, the dress swirling as he did so.

Our faces sat millimetres from one another, and his eyes hooded as he glanced down. The bust of the dress pushed my chest up, revealing much more than I would have chosen to, and the waist sat snug, pulling me in to give the illusion of an hourglass shape.

'We need to keep moving,' he murmured.

'Go then,' I said quietly, not moving an inch.

He grabbed my chin and pulled my face up toward him. 'Trust me when I say I will continue this as soon as we're out of here.'

I didn't need to question what he was wanting to continue, because as soon as he pulled back and walked away from me, his own body gave me the answers.

I smirked to myself and followed behind him, nervous energy coursing through me.

We ran through more and more winding halls, and I was impressed with his sense of direction.

He stopped dead in front of an all white door that had a similar iridescence to that of a pearl.

He placed his hand against the door, and it swung open, revealing a familiar room.

The room from Cyrus' vision. Where Cain had been taken. On the opposite side of the room was a door, the same one he had been taken through, and beside me was the very point where Cyrus had been pinned to the wall by his Father and then beaten.

I had assumed the vision had been an entrance into the mansion, a foyer if you will, not a single room.

Cyrus dropped to the floor and ripped a floorboard from the ground, pulling something out from beneath it.

A silver key.

I turned to leave, but he hissed at me to stay.

'You don't really think it's this one do you?'

'Yes?' I asked, unsure why this was a ridiculous conclusion.

He shook his head and used the key to open a drawer on the large bureau at the side of the room. From inside there, he pulled out a much, much larger golden key, with a ruby encrusted at the top.

I realised why he had scoffed at my assumption.

He hurried to put everything back together, and we scampered out of the room, both of us buzzing with adrenaline that we had what we needed and hadn't been caught.

We turned the corner and Cyrus ushered me past a large mirror. My reflection looked alien. I looked magical.

My red hair complimented the colour of my dress as if it was custom made for me, and the white panel on the front made my blue eyes glow. I never realised how much colour was in my features until this moment.

The dress fell perfectly to my feet, and in all senses, I looked like a princess.

'Yes. You look enchanting. Now keep moving,' Cyrus said, but I detected a hint of playfulness in his tone.

I blushed and carried on toward the backdoor we were to exit out of, before something caught my eye.

A large banner hanging over the door, with Cyrus' face on it.

Help us find our missing heir, it read.

A girl's face sat on the other side. She looked around my age, with jet black hair and dark brown eyes. Her skin was darker than Cyrus', and tears streaked down her cheeks. In her hands, she held a photo of her and Cyrus. Her hand…that had a ring on the fourth finger. Her other hand sat caressing her swollen stomach.

I refused to accept what this meant, but then I read the statement issued below her face.

I need my husband. The father of the next heir of Fire. Please, if you know anything, step forward and you will be rewarded.

Cyrus had a wife. A pregnant wife.

Chapter 12

It all made sense.

Cyrus had always said he wanted to be free from his responsibilities. Did he really mean free from his responsibilities as a husband and father? Was this why he always reserved himself?

How he had played me.

I looked at him in shock, tears pricking my eyes. I had a sudden urge to rip the fabric from my body. My skin crawled beneath his wife's dress, and I felt sick at the fact I had taken pleasure from his reaction only a moment before.

How stupid I must have been to believe he had felt anything at all. How naive to think this cat and mouse game we played was really about sexual tension and desire. He had all of that and more at home. He only needed me for my blood.

'Kaimana…it's not at all what it looks like,' he began.

'Oh, well, I think it is, Cyrusall,' a rough voice boomed from behind me.

I spun around. Reginald Rayos.

'I'm so glad you've returned, son. I was beginning to think you were dead,' Reginald stated, seeming like he didn't care at all.

Cyrus said nothing. His entire demeanor seemed to have shrunk, and I watched the effect his father had over him as he avoided his gaze.

Reginald Rayos was tall, 6ft 5, olive skinned like Cyrus, and had combed over brown hair, and a short stubble along his sharp jaw. He was incredibly muscular, his white shirt was strained over his biceps, and the buttons seemed to be hanging on for dear life across his chest.

His eyes were an even deeper brown than Cyrus' and they stared at me, amused.

'And who is this lovely lady? I don't believe we've met before,' he remarked, holding his hand out toward me.

I clasped it delicately, and held eye contact resolutely.

'Jazlean King,' I answered, nodding my head down in respect.

He raised an eyebrow that told me he believed nothing.

'Let's go, Father. Jazlean you can go home. Thank you for your help,' Cyrus gave me a bow, and gestured out the door.

I frowned at him. I wasn't going anywhere.

'No,' interrupted Reginald. 'She can stay. You need to fill me in as to your whereabouts, and I'm sure she can help.'

I smiled sweetly.

'I would be honoured.'

'It's settled then. Come now,' Reginald smiled, ushering us back toward his study.

Cyrus shot me a look, his usual look; brows furrowed and jaw clenched.

I didn't bother to express anything back to him.

We reached the door to the study, and he opened it up, waiting for us to step inside. I stepped in first and tried to glance around as though I was appreciating the space. A space I had *definitely* never seen before.

'So, boy, what happened?' Reginald asked gruffly, sitting down in a large leather chair behind the bureau.

Cyrus said nothing and only stared at the ground. I fiddled with my hands nervously. Why wasn't he coming up with something?

'I thought as much. Your mother was sure you had been kidnapped, taken by some ruffian looking to extort us, but I told her otherwise. I told her that I would not put it past her only son to leave her childless,' Reginald chuckled, though without humour.

Reginald started toward Cyrus, fists clenched. The flinch in Cyrus' stature, and his acceptance of his fate enraged me, and despite how much he had hurt me, I did not want to see him beaten.

'Cyrus is not your only son,' I said calmly.

'Excuse me?' he said, stopping to turn and glare at me.

'I said, Reggie, that Cyrus is not your only son. Unless, of course, Cain was never yours to begin with,' I replied, keeping my voice level, masking the anger I felt toward this man. Images of him callously sending a young boy off to slaughter and terrorising his other son and wife, played in front of me. Cyrus had shown me only a brief glimpse of his father's behaviour, and yet it was enough to ignite something buried deep within me.

'You DARE to speak to ME like that, girl?' Reginald boomed.

I held his eye and kept my chin up, refusing to cower under his gaze. What was he going to do? Kill me? After my actions these last few days, my fate was sealed regardless and I was not going to back down to this man. Cyrus remained introverted, but was now peering through the fringe of his brown curls to watch the encounter.

'I'll teach you to show respect to your betters,' Reginald cried.

He sent a winding snake of magma around me, before cooling it enough to harden and lock me in place.

I began to feel panic. Maybe he would kill me.

'Better? And in what way are you my better? Because you prey on those weaker than you? Take down someone your own size and then you might have a leg to stand on,' I taunted. I had a secret suspicion that angering him would cause him to resort to violence, which might finally make Cyrus act.

'I am superior to you in EVERY way! Now shut your oversized gob before I burn it from your face!' he yelled, before using his fist to strike me across the face.

I tasted blood on my tongue, and wondered for a moment if he had busted my lip. Nope, blood was dripping down from my eyebrow where his fist had connected.

Cyrus immediately snapped his head up and stepped in front of me, bracing his hands for a fight. I smiled through bloody lips in satisfaction and winked at Reginald.

'Tough guy,' I chuckled under my breath.

'You care for the girl then, eh?' Reginald asked Cyrus, apparently quite puzzled at the prospect.

Cyrus continued to remain silent.

'I guess you should take a few blows in her place then, don't you?' he smiled connivingly.

And as fast as lightning, he punched Cyrus in the ribs so hard I heard a crack, and he dropped to the floor, winded and writhing in pain. Reginald continued to kick his back, spine and ribs, laughing maniacally, his face an awful picture of malevolence. He bent down and picked Cyrus up by the collar, lifting his limp body into the air. I struggled incessantly against the restraints he had built, but to no avail. This was not what I had intended. Why wasn't he fighting back?

Just as Reginald was about to slam Cyrus back against the wall, I did the only thing I could think of. I wiggled my fingertips beneath the stone and managed to poke a couple free. Using them as my weapons, I sent as much water as I could emit directly into Reginald's face and he dropped Cyrus in shock. He wheeled to look at me, and I stopped shooting him.

'Picked yourself up a Water whore then, eh? Maybe you aren't as useless as I thought. Be sure to dump her back where you found her after you make use of it,' he sneered.

Cyrus suddenly roared, and black flames emanated from every inch of his skin, directed straight toward Reginald. I blinked in surprise, and the heat from them crumbled away the rock holding me in place, and I dropped down, ready to help him.

I looked toward Cyrus and noticed his eyes had gone a blazing red, just as they had that day in no-man's land and I felt anxious as to whether he would be able to control this.

Nonetheless, I created a barricade of water to protect Cyrus from his father's snaking magma, sizzling through it as soon as it tried to grab him. The water under my control boiled and steamed from the contact, but I drew on the power from my amethyst to hold it steady, grateful for those brief lessons from Abigail despite the way our association had taken a dark turn.

Reginald finally leapt through the jet black fire and grabbed Cyrus by the throat.

'I had felt it was a pity, but now I'm glad my shadow soldier didn't kill you. I get the pleasure of doing it myself,' Reginald growled.

Cyrus suddenly stopped his attack, and I held the water still, ready to defend him.

'*Your* shadow soldier?' he asked quietly.

'Are you hurt? Do you feel betrayed, son?' Reginald spat. 'Well, now you know how I felt when my heir abandoned my DISTRICT!'

Cyrus had stopped fighting entirely, and his eyes were full of sadness and questions he daren't ask. Reginald was distracted, relishing in the hurt of his first born son, and I used the opportunity to wield both my elements to give us a chance to run.

The fire and water fired out in beautiful harmony, and I focused on the energy of my amethyst to amplify the power. I channelled it directly into my magic, and soon felt another source pushing at the barriers of my magic, an energy I recognised as I had harnessed it before. Cyrus' tiger's eye.

I used both of our strengths and pushed myself harder than I ever had.

Cyrus was now deflated, but continued to barrage his father in flames, and Reginald was firing one arm at us both, trying to immobilise us in stone, but our combined power was overtaking his attempts, bit by bit.

Our magic seemed to flow together like yin and yang, and without needing to communicate, we wrapped an entire wall of Cyrus' dark flames around Reginald, blinding him, before I joined him, controlling lava to take their place. As soon as the lava was formed, I blasted water at it to solidify Reginald inside.

Soon, he was fully encapsulated and all of a sudden, my magic felt considerably weakened. It seemed as though I had been drained from the inside out, and a hollowness wracked through my bones.

I stopped wielding and panted. Cyrus immediately rushed to my side and allowed me to lean against him.

'We need to move quickly. He'll be out of there any minute,' he urged.

He was right. I could hear the blaze Reginald was creating inside to crumble his way out.

He supported me up, and never letting go of my arm, we ran out of the mansion and into the desolate wilderness beyond.

Chapter 13

We ran as fast as my legs would go. I knew Cyrus could
easily pull ahead, but he stayed by my side, holding me
up.

'Cyrus!' a lilting voice called from behind.

He snapped his head around and ran toward the voice.

I turned to watch and saw as he ran into a raven haired
woman's arms. She was crying and stroking his hair. He
easily had 2ft on her, but she stretched up to him anyway.
I felt a pang of hurt in my heart as I thought of the pleas
from his wife on the banner.

But as Cyrus pulled back, I noticed this woman looked
much older. She had many fine lines, softening her
features and giving her a gentle countenance. Her hands
shook vigorously.

I drew in closer to hear their conversation. It was clear
that they had a close, loving bond. I felt a sense of
pleasure that Cyrus had at least one family member at his
side. I thought of Paula, and the image of her smiling face

in my mind sent pain waving through me. How I missed her.

'I'm so sorry, Mother. You know I hate leaving you with him, but I have to find Cain, I just have to,' he said, almost pleadingly.

'Oh, sweet boy. I know. It's too late now anyway, the damage is done. Your father will never let you live if you return,' she whispered, sobbing.

'I don't care what he does to me. It's you I worry about.'

'Don't worry about me. I know who I married, and I know how to hide from him,' she smiled at him sadly.

Cyrus pulled her in again for a tight embrace, and her eyes finally rested on me.

Her voice dropped to a low murmur in Cyrus' ear, and I could no longer hear the exchange between them. I glanced around nervously, conscious of Reginald catching up with us.

Cyrus finally came jogging back over to me, reciting words under his breath, his mother watching us silently.

'Reach the lava falls, right, below the haunted oak,' he repeated, over and over.

He said nothing else, and wrapped his arm around my waist, ready to help me keep moving, but I shook him off.

'Kaimana, you're drained,' he stated, confused. 'Let me help you.'

'I'm fine.'

He cast a final look at his mother, who was now wielding some sort of magic that rippled through the air, and we continued moving forward.

'She's casting a concealment spell,' he explained. 'It won't last long against my father, but it gives us long enough to get to where we need to go. Reach the lava falls, right, below the haunted oak.' His words were like a mantra he was clinging onto.

'Won't he know what she's done?' I asked, concerned for her life.

'Yes, he will. But she's promised me she's going to do the spell and run. I told her how to get into no-man's land. She can camp there until I come back for her.'

I didn't say it out loud, but I highly doubted she would be able to escape the district alive. Even if she could, there's no way Reginald would allow both his heir and his wife to be missing.

We followed the directions Cyrus' mother had given him in silence, an unspoken understanding between us that talking right now would take too much energy and time that we no longer had. We passed an extraordinary display of what looked like the waterfalls from home, but pouring blindingly bright lava instead, a small ache of longing formed inside my chest but I took a deep breath and shook it off. We reached the 'haunted' oak tree shortly before nightfall.

'Why is it haunted?' I asked.

'People are deposited inside the trunk, and then trapped in there with a blocking spell when they're executed,' he explained grimly. 'Fire signs can't feel normal pain like you, so the pain has to come from within your flesh, and what better way than being cramped, starving and eaten alive by Spires?'

'Spires?'

'Spires are a type of…I don't know what creatures you have where you're from for comparison, but they're slimy, wriggling beings. They're tiny, with thousands of little legs and have no teeth, so they enter your body through all your orifices and gnaw away at you from the inside out,' he explained again.

I shuddered, and wished I hadn't asked.

He felt around the base of the dead tree, and then seemed to find what he was looking for, as he burnt away the roots on one side.

I peered down from behind him, and saw a very strangely shaped rock looking back at me.

'Is that what we're looking for?' I asked.

'Yep,' he replied, putting the key into the hole. It slotted in perfectly.

'Clever, isn't it? Make an execution site 'haunted' so no one dares to come near, and hide the entrance to The Centre within,' he remarked, watching as the key began to emit a glowing light from the ruby.

I nodded, though I wasn't sure I agreed.

A rumble beneath the surface caused us to look at one another in alarm. The ground shook and fractures spread across the surface.

'Is this normal?' I asked in a shaky voice.

He didn't reply and only clutched onto my arm as my legs wobbled against the shaking ground. He looked around, frowning, and his eyes focused hard as he seemed to spot something in the distance that I didn't.

A narrow tunnel finally appeared below us, and just as I was about to question whether this was the entrance, I felt a sharp shove on my shoulders and tumbled down into it, landing in a heap on the damp, rocky ground a few metres below.

Cyrus jumped in after me, key in hand. The tunnel entrance was closing, and I realised why Cyrus had wasted no time in pushing me through. Sharp, wiry, steel claws were poking through, followed by blazing red eyes. The metal monsters. Metallums.

They chittered some sort of call to one another, and one of them with a tongue as long as my entire body emitted an ear piercing shriek as it attempted to hook us on its barbs.

The noises drowned out as the hole sealed itself shut, and I tore my gaze from where it had been, my eyes searching frantically for Cyrus in the darkness.

'Illuminare,' I heard him mutter, and felt relief wash over me.

Small flames now lined the circular area that held us, and continued down a pathway to our left.

He stalked down it, not looking at me for some unbeknownst reason. I followed suit, feeling the heat from the flames brush against my ankles beneath my dress, and realised his gifted power had expired.

～

We travelled along the same path for what I was sure had been hours. My feet ached, and I had begun to feel claustrophobic in the damp tunnel.

We soon reached a point which inclined, and excitement, fear and anticipation flooded through me. This had to be the end of our journey in this godforsaken district, and I would be more than happy to leave and never return to its unrelenting landscape.

We emerged upward and glanced around our new surroundings.

We were on a beach. A beach surrounded by black water, and littered with debris. Much like the land in no-man's land, but far more sinister.

Four sets of towering iron gates stood between the circular rock face which segregated the beach from The Centre.

Despite the fact the area seemed desolate, sounds reverberated through the air. Chittering birds came from above us, though the creatures were invisible in the treetops. It was not yet dark, but the sun was beginning to set and the rays seemed to be entirely absorbed by the blackness of the sea.

I looked toward The Centre. I could barely see anything beyond the towering mountain faces, and I wondered what it would look like once we reached the inside. I had spent my life in Water hearing terrible rumours, and now that I was here, they were running wildly in the forefront of my mind.

I thought back to my preconceptions about the Fire district, and how they had been entirely wrong. How would my ideas of The Centre fare to the truths that lied within? Would we encounter yet another grotesque monster, ready to eat us? How much more would I uncover about the world we lived in? I had been naive to the magic all around me, and wondered if the lessons I had learnt would uphold as we progressed. My entire journey had taught me things I had never even thought of, and I felt wary that The Centre was likely to be the pinnacle of those.

I looked toward the water longingly. I felt an overtaking urge to go to it, to finally submerge my limbs that had been land ridden for too long. Ignoring it, I jogged to catch up with Cyrus, who was now heading towards the mountain sides that encircled The Centre.

'What are we looking for now?' I called out.
'I don't know,' he admitted, a sigh escaping him. 'I thought the coordinates would mean there was a specific purpose to leave from Fire, but I have seen nothing to explain why.'
I looked around, eyes sharp for anything that didn't match the environment, which might tell us why we were directed here, specifically.
Skeletons of unknown, large creatures seemed to lie routinely near the water's edge, and I approached one curiously. Looking to my left and right, they continued to appear periodically, each one different.

The one I approached was only distinguishable when I stood below it, my dress muddying in the water.

A lion? I had seen some animals in books in the library, and this was an exact replica.

I noticed above the lion skeleton there lay an abnormally shaped bone, forming a 'V'.

I picked it up and turned it around in my palms, confused by the shape. It fit nowhere in the lion's skeleton. Where had this lion even come from?

I whistled to Cyrus, and he stopped rummaging through the sand to head over to me. I passed him the 'V' shaped bone and he also looked perplexed.

I walked a few metres left and observed the next skeleton. Except it didn't look like an animal at all, it looked like a woman's skull, what remained of her hair falling beside her. Another oddly shaped bone sat above her, 'VI'.

Sudden realisation hit me, and I gasped audibly.

'VI' meant six. The sixth zodiac, Virgo.

I hurried around the island, confirming my suspicions, and Cyrus called after me.

'What have you found? I don't understand!'

I ignored him and kept running along the water's edge, the hem of my dress trailing behind me.

Libra, Scorpio, Sagittarius, Capricorn, Aquarius…and Pisces.

I stopped at the bones marking out the shapes of two fish, and gingerly picked up the 'XII' bone above them.

'The twelfth zodiac,' I murmured to myself.

But what did this mean? What was the purpose of having each of the zodiacs displayed across the beach?

I turned back to run to Cyrus, to explain what I had figured out, but before words could escape me, the bones that remained in both of our hands began to shake.

We locked eyes in bewilderment, and the bones continued to rattle. A sudden wave rose up like a sheet of darkness, a few metres behind Cyrus, and crashed against the shore, another one doing the same thing behind me. I watched intently, and as the waves retreated, the bones of our zodiac signs, Leo and Pisces, had been washed away into the black sea.

'They're the zodiacs,' I explained hurriedly, 'from the first round to the twelfth. You're holding the fifth, Leo, and me, Pisces.'

'Oh, I see,' he replied, brows pressed together in confusion.

'I don't know what it means, or why ours have just been washed off the beach, but there must be something else of importance around here.'

He gazed around, before fixing his stare on a singular point of the mountainside.

'Come,' he barked, running across the beach and towards it.

I rolled my eyes and followed, irritated by his demands but curious to see what he had seen. He was usually the quicker of the two of us, despite me not wanting to admit it, and I hoped he had figured out what we needed to do next.

He trailed his fingers along the rock face, his eyes closed, and then…ran into the mountain? Cyrus completely disappeared from view, and I frowned at the surface in front of me. Where had he gone? How had he just run through this solid mountain? It looked formidable and I could not quite believe my eyes, despite knowing that his powers were immense.

I tried to do as he had done and feel along the ridges, unsure what I was looking for, when an arm burst out in front of my face from inside of it.

I screamed and hit the flailing hand.

It grabbed a hold of the front panel of my dress and yanked me toward the mountainside. I braced, ready for the hit I was sure to take straight to the face, and then emerged through the other side.

'Oh,' I breathed, looking around the damp, dripping cave that Cyrus had just pulled me into.

'Concealment spell,' he explained. 'I could see the faint ripple of magic from the water's edge as we were so far back from it, and just had to get closer to find the spot that had been hidden.'

'Right,' I replied with nonchalance, as all this knowledge of new spells and teachings were becoming commonplace to me. 'Where are we?'

'We're halfway between the beach and The Centre. This can't be what we were supposed to find, but it's where we've ended up for now. Let's see if it leads anywhere.' He marked where we had entered by charring the rocks that sat haphazardly in front of it and then we walked next to one another down the dark path, droplets of water echoing as they splashed onto the ground.

'Cyrus?'

'Yes?'

I sighed, not knowing how to begin asking what I wanted to ask.

'Your wife…is she really pregnant?' I asked in a quiet voice.

He looked at me as we continued walking, but I kept my gaze on the floor.

'She is pregnant. She isn't my wife. We're engaged,' he sighed.

I nodded, feigning disinterest.

'But the baby isn't mine, and the engagement was arranged. We don't care for one another,' he continued.

I stopped dead in my tracks and finally looked back at him.

'What?'

'My father arranged the engagement, the same as all the heirs, but we decided early on that she could continue seeing her former flame. Unfortunately, they were careless and became pregnant, so my father had to spin the story that the child is mine. I hate it. Not only do I have to keep up this pretence that I have a child on the way, but the real father must be devastated. I never knew his name for his own safety from my father, but Annalise was destroyed over it,' he said, shaking his head.

'Annalise…Is that her name?' I asked cautiously, fearing many more details would only hurt me further.

'Yes,' he answered. 'You've asked me before why I insist I cannot kiss you, why I cannot go further than declaring myself with words. Well, I have two reasons. One: I know it's nonsensical, and I know she has done far worse, but engagements are an extremely serious thing in Fire, and I feel a sense of disloyalty and as though I would be betraying her, despite me holding no loving affection for her. Two: you scare me. I often feel like we take a step forward, but then you react to things in a way that makes me realise we're five steps behind where I thought we were. I know I've given you little reason to trust me, I know we have come from a violent place, but over time my feelings toward you changed from this confused suspicion, to a desire to protect you, to hold you and never let you go. Kaimana, in all my life, I have never felt like I had any purpose beyond the one I was born for. You've changed that. I know I haven't behaved in a way that might have shown this, but you must understand I couldn't. I had to withdraw in every moment where I wanted to proceed closer. I couldn't risk you seeing the real me, not when I am unable to be what you need. And I know you don't trust me, I know you feel as though I'm using you, and so I always retreat myself from your embrace. I will not have you wondering if my kiss is because I wish to gain something from you. And because of this, I know we never shall. You will never look at me the same as I do you, and I accept this. I have done it to myself,' Cyrus spoke in a way that suggested he felt he had already sealed his fate.

Tears fell freely from my eyes at his words. A mixture of hurt, confusion and desire swirled in my mind, and I had no idea how to separate them from one another. Ultimately, he was right. I knew I had grown to want him. How I had spent so much time thinking of his warmth, his gentle touch despite his hardness. I had been so severely in denial for so long. It was cemented the moment the news of his engagement caused me pain. He was desirable to anyone with the gift of sight, and I'd argue even those without, but I always found something in the back of my mind warning me not to trust him. Whether it was because I had never heard the words he had spoken from another, and so I couldn't accept them, or whether it was because he wasn't being honest, I didn't know. But regardless, I couldn't argue with him, tell him how wrong he was, because he was right. And it killed me.

His hand raised to wipe the tears from my cheek and I leaned into it, accepting my vulnerability for the first time.

I struggled to find the words, a correct response to give, but our momentary silence was interrupted by a hoarse, croaking voice.

'You've found me at last. What took you so long?'

In an instant, we both dropped our hands in front of us, his blazing in fire and mine swirling water rapidly.

'Illuminare!' Cyrus cried, and the entire space around us became illuminated by dancing flames suspended in the air.

An iron cage sat at the end of the passageway, a hunched figure sitting in the centre of it.

We glanced at each other and nodded, slowly advancing toward the figure.

'Who are you?' I asked loudly.

A low chuckle reached our ears, but no response.

Cyrus flicked his wrist, and a trail of fire extended from him to the figure.

An unimaginably skinny, drooping fae sat, lit up by the flames. His face seemed to hang from his bones, and his eyes were clouded white. Chains wrapped around his body, though he could have slipped from them easily. He had no hair other than a few wiry strands hanging from the top of his head. His shaking fingers lifted into the air, his nails long and sharp, and he beckoned us closer.

'She said: who are you?' Cyrus demanded through gritted teeth, shaking his head at me as I moved closer.

Call me crazy, but I didn't feel like we were in danger.

I ignored his warning and moved closer cautiously, ready to send an onslaught of water toward the hallowed figure.

'Kaimana,' the voice croaked.

I stopped my approach and saw Cyrus' eyes widen just as mine did.

'I have been waiting for you. You and Rayos,' the voice continued. 'Forgive me, for I cannot see except in my mind.'

'What do you mean, you've been waiting? How do you know who we are?' Cyrus demanded.

I watched as the man's entirely white eyes glazed over.

'You needn't use your powers on me,' the man chuckled. 'I have no access to my magic to pose a threat to you.'

It suddenly clicked into place.

'He's a seer,' I murmured to Cyrus.

'Well done, Kaia. Now, I trust you brought the bones?' the figure asked.

I started as he used my nickname so casually, as though he had known me for years. I looked at the bone in my spare hand and the other in one of Cyrus'.

'Who are you? Why do you want them?' I asked.

'Surely, you must know who I am by now. You have been reading my journal for an awfully long time, sweet girl.'

Chapter 14

I dropped the hold on my power immediately and took
several step forwards, shaking off Cyrus' grip as I moved.
'Shadow Atlas?' I whispered.

He nodded, smiling a toothless smile.

'Albert?' Cyrus asked from behind me. 'Albert Kersey?'

'Oh, no, dear boy. Albert was also imprisoned, but he is
not Shadow Atlas. I am. And I am Zephyr Oberton.'

I felt as though I could have screamed. Zephyr?
Infamous dictator and creator of the districts?

'Impossible,' Cyrus whispered, though his expression told
me he was just as unsure as I was.

'Quite possible, my children. Did you know I was the
most powerful seer of my time? I'm sure someone has
taken that title from me now, but it was how I was able to
write that journal. How I knew one day, all these years
later, you would both find half. The halves would bring

you together in chaos, but ultimately, would lead you here,' Zephyr spoke.

Words failed us, unable to fathom what Zephyr was telling us.

'The bones, dear?' Zephyr asked me again.

'What do you need them for?' Cyrus asked suspiciously.

'I can see that you do not trust me, nor even want to believe me. I know a horrible tale was spun about me, but it is simply untrue,' Zephyr sighed.

'You are the cause for everything,' Cyrus hissed. 'The districts, the segregation, The Centre!'

Before I could cut in to tell Cyrus to let him explain, my vision was taken from me and I found myself looking through the eyes of a man.

I knew they would come for me, eventually.

A large group of fae descended upon me, battling against my four streams of magic. A hooded figure stood in the centre of them all, untouched.

'Why are you doing this?' I cried. 'There is nothing to gain from this abuse of power!'

'I have to disagree, Zephyr. Your power will be enough to fuel our universe for centuries. I would be a fool if I didn't capitalise on that,' the hooded figure replied darkly.

I continued to send a swirling combination of fire, water, twisting vines and vortexes of air toward the fae surrounding me. I would never submit.

Fae began falling to the ground one by one as I focused in on precision attacks.

A torrent of water blasted two miles backwards, an almighty blaze caused horrified shrieks to come from a group of five as their flesh melted from their bones, a thorn ridden vine whipped across three necks, tearing their throats, and a crackling tornado, rippling with energy, finally eliminated the last two, the wind so powerful their limbs were detached from their bodies.

It didn't take long until only one stood in front of me. This mysterious fae who had plagued my visions.

He had learnt how to mess with my sight, how to manipulate the visions, so I was never 100% sure what he was going to do next.

'Enough!' he bellowed, brandishing a small, golden haired girl from behind his back.

'Seryn!' I rushed toward her, but was promptly stopped by a swirl of dark shadow which held me in place.

'What magic is this?' I asked, disgusted.

'Only those who can access the dark realm are strong. None of your elemental magic can touch me,' he sneered.

He held Seryn in the air, and she wailed. My precious daughter.

'Father!' she cried. 'Father save me!'

I fought tirelessly against the darkness surrounding me, but gained no freedom.

I roared in agony as I watched the cloaked man lift Seryn high above him with the same darkness that restrained me.

Her little frocked dress swung madly as she kicked and screamed, her small face mottled with tears.

A crack, a snap, and her lifeless body fell to the ground, her neck bent unnaturally.

I let out a long scream and I felt a draining sensation from my chest. I didn't care to find out what it was. My eyes were fixed on

*the young girl who had only experienced a few years in this world,
failed by me.*

*My entire body heaved with sobs and yet I was still unable to
move from the restraints that held me. I looked up in fury, ready
to make my final kill.*

*The hooded figure simply stood there laughing, and I roared yet
again.*

*'I will not rest until you suffer the most excruciating death you
can imagine. Over long days and weeks I shall pull your insides
out through your mouth, before healing you and doing it all
again,' I promised.*

*'You shan't do any such thing, Oberton. You have no power,' he
cackled.*

No power? Of course I had power!

*He held up a bone, completely straight and about six inches in
length.*

*'I have your power now. And you will be the one to suffer. You
shall live forever, and so shall your power, in this bone of the
original Aries.'*

'The original zodiacs?' I asked, my heart thrumming.

*'That's right. Now, allow my friends to escort you to your new
home, whilst I shape the world,' he smiled sadistically.*

*I thrashed and fought, desperately trying to grab him as he turned
from me. I would avenge Seryn no matter what it takes. No
matter the cost, I will ensure I take revenge in her name.*

My vision returned to me, and I gasped, falling sideways
into Cyrus. He steadied me and kept a hand on my back
before speaking to Zephyr again.

'The districts weren't formed in that vision. But if you were imprisoned, how did you create them?' he asked.

I shook my head. Even I understood what had happened. Zephyr's power had been taken from him, able to be transferred as he exerted such an outburst of emotion. The cloaked fae had created the districts and everything since then, using his stored power. What I didn't understand was the mention of the 'original zodiacs'.

'He didn't create them,' I answered. 'But what are the original zodiacs? What is the significance of these bones?' My mind was still scrambling to piece it all together.

'The original zodiacs were the first fae to ever be born to this world. They each fell from stars, each one from a different constellation of the zodiacs. 12 fae and 12 sources of power.

They were supposed to be eternal, but once the world became populated enough to survive on its own, they were reclaimed by the stars. The graves you saw are the remains of their true form,' Zephyr explained.

'And they're just laying out there for all to see?' Cyrus asked, the scepticism apparent in his tone.

'No. They only become visible when one of their true descendants is present. It is rumoured the district leaders were chosen as they were direct descendants of their sign. Which means, Cyrus, you are a descendant of Apollo, the original Leo.'

I looked at Cyrus in shock, thinking that it did make sense. Cyrus was exceptionally powerful. He had healing powers and was able to perform verbal spells, not just cast elemental magic.

'So what's the significance?' I asked again, trying to withhold the frustration from my voice. 'Why are these bones important to us now? I understand they must be a power source, but why do we need it to save Cain?'

'There are some answers I cannot give you. If I interfere with your journey too much, it will not succeed. I will, however, tell you that the bones of your signs will be essential to fight the battle you have facing you. The hooded man still lives, still rules The Centre, and he holds the bones of Aries, not only storing my power, but the power of Ares also,' Zephyr warned.

'So how do we get into The Centre from here?' Cyrus demanded.

'You can't,' Zephyr replied simply.

'Well, then we will have to find our own way,' Cyrus said sternly.

He strode off back toward where we had come from, but I didn't follow. I didn't know why he was being so pig headed and difficult, but Zephyr had answers, many answers we needed.

'Don't fret. He's struggling with the news of his ancestry,' Zephyr smiled.

I gave a reflexive small smile back and decided to ask what I had been wanting to ask since he revealed his identity.

'Why did you choose me and Cyrus? Why were we supposed to find your journal?'

'I didn't choose you, my dear. My visions are gifts from the gods themselves, so if my vision showed me you finding the journal, then the gods chose you. Not me,' he answered.

I thought over this and imagined the zodiac gods up in the sky, discussing me and Cyrus. I don't think they quite realised what they were getting into.

'How can you get out of there?' I asked guiltily. Something about Zephyr was familiar. I felt as though I could trust him and yet he remained trapped in his cage.

'There's no way out without my power,' he said sadly. 'My power was used to create this cage and only my power can release me.'

'How were you even imprisoned here? What was the ritual you spoke of in your diary? Why did the cloaked fae want to create the districts?' I rattled, years of unanswered questions firing from my tongue impatiently.

He chuckled. 'You are an inquisitive one. I was imprisoned because I lost my power. The only one that can never be stripped from me is my gift of sight. The cloaked fae was able to enchant my soul to render me eternal, and the prison is sealed with my own magic. The ritual I spoke of was the ritual I had to complete in order to weaken the districts. My sight told me that the districts were coming, months prior. So I left my wife at home and dedicated myself to travelling across Elorial, leaving significant magical impacts that would leave a dent in any other spells cast there. This is what formed the passageways between districts. Of course, the cloaked man had no idea I was doing this and so had no thought to rectify it. I do not know why he sought to fracture our world. I never spoke with him long enough to find out.'

I thought over his words and felt a sense of satisfaction as answers began clicking in place in my mind. I almost felt star struck. How many years had I spent reading his inner thoughts?

We were taught that Zephyr Oberton was a villain. A fae who was so cruel, and so mad with power, he fractured the surface of the planet in order to exert control. Yet, the man I saw in front of me was no more than someone whose livelihood had been stolen from him, and abused for his gifts. Someone broken. I knew it may have been naive to believe him so quickly, but something inside me was enforcing the notion that he could be trusted. I decided to follow my instincts, as they had gotten me this far.

'I'm sorry about your daughter,' I said quietly.

Zephyr simply nodded gratefully.

'Is there truly no way to get to The Centre?' I asked.

'Of course there is. But not from here, not from this point. You would have to enter through the gates,' he said.

'So how do we get in? They're not just going to open the gates for us,' I replied.

'No, no they won't. District leaders get in because of their status, but regular fae can only enter if they hold more than one element. This is tested through your blood,' he explained.

'So me and Cyrus need to blood share? Then we can get in?' I asked excitedly. We were so close now.

He sighed and shook his head.

'I can't tell you anymore, Kaimana.'

I nodded and took that as confirmation. We needed to exchange elements and then when our blood was tested, we would have enough to enter.

'I'll be back,' I said earnestly to Zephyr.

'I know,' he sighed.

I hurried to find Cyrus, to explain what we needed to do to save Cain, and my parents.

I found him sitting, back against the damp wall, head in hands.

'Cyrus, I got so much information from Zephyr. I know how we need to get in! If we just exchange a little...' I began.

'Stop! Kaimana, you are not seeing the big picture here, as usual,' he interrupted. 'You realise my own father sent a life sucking, torturous, demonic creature after me, right?'

I nodded, biting my lip as feelings of guilt and sympathy washed over me as the weight of what had passed finally beared down upon Cyrus.

'Good. So then you understand he is going to notice the key to The Centre passage is missing, and knows exactly where we're going, and may send more,' he finished.

'I'm quite aware that's a possibility. So is being killed on sight when we reach The Centre gate. So is starving to death as neither of us have eaten since we left the Water district. There's a hell of a lot of ways in which we may not come out of this, but that didn't stop the man I met in no-man's land, determined to save his little brother. The fae I met was merciless. He did what he had to do in order to protect his brother, and would never have stopped at the actions of his father,' I replied brashly, his hint at my ignorance irritating me.

'Don't act like you're doing everything for Cain,' he laughed. 'We both know you're just dying to see if your parents are in there.'

His words stung and yet instead of retaliating as I normally would have done, I tried to remain sensitive to his situation.

'Yes, you're right. I do want to see if my parents can be saved, because frankly, who wouldn't? But if they aren't there, then I'm still here with you to save Cain.'

He looked up at me, his expression surprised, as though he had expected a fight.

A few silent moments passed before he spoke again.

'My father wasn't always this way, you know? Until I was around five years old, he was as much an ordinary parent as anyone else's. Of course, I had media training and certain responsibilities other children did not, and I had to learn to control my power much earlier than most, but he was…kind. I felt as though he cared for me as more than just an heir. As I grew up, he slowly revealed himself. And I knew his former behaviour had been an act because of the way he treated my mother. I soon realised he only showed me patience in case my untrained mouth revealed something it shouldn't, and because I had not yet mastered how to heal myself for the public eye. Even so, knowing who he is, I never truly believed he would kill me. The gods know he threatened to, but I never really believed him, especially after Cain was taken.

Afterall, who would become the heir? Sure, they could make another, but how suspicious would that look? I guess we are all wrong sometimes.'

My heart saddened for him. I had no parents and no money, but I would much rather have it that way than have a father like Reginald.

'My parents died…or disappeared…when I was six years old. I hardly remember them,' I began to tell him, feeling as though I owed him some reciprocation. 'All I can really recall are some faint memories of them talking to me, but not really enough to go on. I was first passed to their best friends, Maria and Thierre Bloom, Zach's parents - the boy you threatened outside my house. They cared for me well. They had known me well enough that they didn't paint me with the same traitorous brush that everyone else did my parents. However, after I was officially orphaned, I had to go into foster care. I spent no more than a few months in each household; no one wanted the traitors' daughter.

The worst place I ever lived was with the Descia family. God, they were awful fae.' I paused for a minute, recalling the sadness, fear and loneliness that nearly overwhelmed me at such a young age and then settled my breathing to continue. 'They used to keep me wrapped in water pretty much all the time, tentacles of it holding me in place. I was held down to my bed to sleep, in my chair to eat, and dragged along behind them whenever they went out. The only times I was granted free will were when I went to school, and then the library. As I got older, I got stronger and could take over control of their tentacles. Me being hot headed, I would send them straight back to the Descias. Of course, they then decided they were unfit to house me and I had to be moved again.'

'Explains why you were trying to flee the district,' Cyrus pointed out. 'And why your combat skills are so advanced,' he said, almost playfully, but with a hint of admiration.

Relieved to have the emotional memories broken, I chuckled gratefully in response and sat down opposite him.

'Zephyr said you were struggling with the news of your ancestry. Isn't it remarkable though? To be a descendant of Apollo?' I said to him gently.

'Zephyr,' he spat as if the name were venomous. 'Don't you think it's odd? He's being held here all this time, the most powerful fae to ever live, and he couldn't take down one measly man? He could just be showing us what he wants us to see. He was probably imprisoned for his treachery!'

I chewed my cheek, not knowing how to say I disagreed without sending him on a rampage. Truly, I didn't even know why I disagreed so heartily. My entire view of him had shifted, and I felt like he was an old friend. I put it down to the fact I had read his journal so many times, I felt as though I knew him personally.

'You saw how it happened. His daughter was killed in front of him. Anyone would probably give up. I truly believe we can trust him. Something about him is just familiar to me,' I said quietly.

Cyrus laughed darkly, shaking his head.

'You are far too trusting. That's how you've ended up here! Because you trusted me enough to stop trying to kill me and in return, I managed to get you to sneak me into Water and now look where we are!' he said angrily.

'Exactly. We are only a few small steps away from where we need to be. I made the decision to trust you and I don't regret it,' I said firmly.

'Except the choice wasn't your own,' he muttered.

'What do you mean?'

A voice carried down to us from Zephyr's prison.

'The boy is trying to tell you he used a mind altering spell on you.'

Chapter 15

I looked at Cyrus in disbelief, not understanding why Zephyr would say something like that. Cyrus didn't meet my eye and pushed past me, back to Zephyr.

He had done *what?*

'You just think you know everything, don't you?' Cyrus yelled, thrusting his arms through the bars, attempting to grasp Zephyr.

'Unfortunately I do,' said Zephyr calmly, not moving and still remaining out of Cyrus' grasp. 'You know that I do.'

My hands shook and I couldn't comprehend the conversation playing out in front of me.

All this time I had believed I was acting of my own accord. Making reckless decisions because I had hidden feelings buried under the layers of distrust. When in reality, the decisions were never mine. Cyrus had stripped me callously of my free will, and humiliated me in the process.

'What the hell is going on?' I whispered.

Cyrus whipped around to look at me, a nervous expression playing on his features.

'You have to understand, I needed you to trust me. I had to get you to move past your hesitation in order to progress. I was never going to hurt you,' Cyrus hurried to explain.

'What are you trying to tell me?' I demanded.

He didn't answer and instead just continued to try to explain himself.

'I rarely used it, or I tried not to at least. I never used it for anything other than your reluctance to help me!'

'You used mind control on me?' I hissed.

'It wasn't mind-control!' Cyrus protested, 'It was more…an influence over your decisions!'

'Like my one to join you here?' I was livid and barely containing my rage.

'No! Well… I don't know. I don't think so. After we left the Water District to head into Fire, I let go of my control over it. I didn't keep hold of it the entire time,' he explained, a hint of desperation breaking through his tone.

'That's the real reason you won't be close to me,' I realised. 'You spouted me all of that bullshit about trust and your fiance, when in actual fact it was because you can't be sure that it isn't just your mind controlling me, making me want you!'

'That's not true,' said Cyrus. 'Everything I told you was the truth. I just knew you would take more persuasion to trust me to come into your home and allow me to find out what I needed to know.'

'I asked myself so many times: why am I still here? Why am I helping you? And all along, it was never really my decision, anyway,' I laughed humorlessly. 'That's why you don't trust Zephyr! You know that he knows these things!'

I whirled around to face Zephyr.

'Anything else I should know?'

'I can't reveal all, dear. You know this,' Zephyr reminded me.

'So there is then, basically. Why don't you tell me yourself?' I asked Cyrus scathingly.

Cyrus had dropped his arms to his sides and now reached out to me. I retreated and didn't allow him to touch me.

'Kaimana, I'm sorry. I promise you there is nothing else, no other reason for you to fear me. I regretted it the moment I cast the spell and nothing will ever make up for it. But I need you to believe that I never wanted to hurt you,' he pleaded.

I laughed again. Believe him? I could never believe another word that came out of his mouth.

'That didn't stop you from doing it again though, did it?' I spat angrily.

Realisation dawned on me and I shook my head at my own stupidity. 'I thought you had a *charisma* charm on you. I even asked you about it, and you lied to my face. You're a coward.'

'Give it to her, Cyrus,' Zephyr said coolly.

Cyrus sighed and shook his head.

'Shut up.'

'Give me what?' I asked.

Cyrus groaned in frustration and then held out a small drawstring bag. I opened it up and saw there were chips of tiger's eye inside.

'What is this?' I asked, irritated.

'Hand me your necklace,' Cyrus said, holding his hand out.

'No.'

'Fine,' Cyrus huffed.

He took the chips into his hand and pressed the same hand holding them, against my amethyst. A red glow emanated from his hand and I watched curiously.

He removed his hand and my amethyst was now imbued with the pieces of tiger's eye. I looked at him expectantly.

'It's tied to my magic now, so no matter what, you can draw on my power as well. You can also access my memories without me granting you access,' he explained, eyes on the ground submissively.

'Why have you given me this?' I demanded.

'Honestly? In case something goes wrong. If we get separated or one of us gets captured… You can draw on me to help you escape. All those officers have two elements, so it seems fair that you have more than one source of power. And if we need to find eachother again, you can see my memories and trace my steps,' he answered.

I knew the gesture was supposed to be kind, thoughtful, whatever you wanted to call it. But to me, it sounded egotistical, self serving and nothing but more manipulation.

He was not going to restore my trust in him that easily now that I had full control of myself, it seemed for the first time since we met.

'Great,' I snapped.

'I'm going to head out and look for some food,' Cyrus sighed.

I waited until he was completely out of sight before I dropped to my knees and wept. I felt violated, undignified, hurt. But more than anything, I felt utterly betrayed.

'Kaimana, stop your tears,' Zephyr's voice rang out to me.

I looked up at him through blurred vision.

'I know you feel betrayed. You and Cyrus were two halves of the same whole. Entirely different, but completely the same. And the one who was supposed to understand your hurt, is now the one causing it. But Kaia, for a moment, place yourself in his shoes. You saw Cain being taken. Did you not feel the desperation? The utter determination to do whatever it takes?' Zephyr asked me.

'Of course I did! I felt the same way about my parents once I realised they could be alive. But I never tried to control Cyrus' decisions,' I said angrily.

'You didn't know the spell. If you knew and could perform the spell, would you not?'

'Of course I wouldn't!' I protested. But I had to admit to myself, it might have been tempting. Back then, when me and Cyrus were insistent on violence, chaos and didn't know one another, if I had needed him to agree with me in order to find my parents, would I have cast a spell to get him to agree? The answer, much as I didn't want to accept it, was yes, I probably would have.

I took a few shuddery breaths and wiped my face roughly with the back of my hand.

I didn't forgive him. I didn't condone his actions and I didn't agree with his reasons. But, as much as I didn't want to, I thought I might understand them.

I nodded to Zephyr and gave him a small smile.

'Go and talk to him. You may feel broken, but I know he feels worse over what he did to you, than he does about even what he has discovered about his father hunting him.'

I sighed. Already, I was feeling sorry for him and it had been no more than twenty minutes. My feelings were absurd. I should bear no sympathy for the man who clearly felt none toward me.

I began heading down the path to find Cyrus, not to console him or to even talk with him, but we needed to continue this. And as I walked on, my stomach growled noisily. I was hungry. We needed to find food and gather our strength so that we could continue our journey.

Kaimana…

I turned back toward Zephyr, but the voice wasn't coming from his direction.

Kaimana…Come to me…

I frowned and stepped through the point Cyrus had marked earlier to allow us back through the concealment spell. I looked all around the beach for the source of the sound.

As I approached the edge of the water, the black inkinesss lapping at the shore eerily, I strained my eyesight to see the defences of the Earth district in the distance.

Towering walls of green encircled the district, and I wondered what lay behind them.

Kaimana, go back to where you belong...

I snapped my head downward. The voice seemed to be coming from...the sea?

I could see nothing, and the surface seemed impenetrable. I took another tiny step forward and let the water wash over my feet. Feeling an intense longing, I stepped in further. How long had it been since I swam? I knew rationally it had only been a couple of days, but my soul felt as though it had been years.

I glanced around quickly, and then dived beneath the surface. No one would miss me for a few minutes while I satisfied my elemental desires.

My dress dragged heavily behind me and a dreamy feeling flooded through me. All my worries, hurt and anxiety seemed to fall away. I could hardly even remember what they were. Thoughts of Cyrus and all that we had gone through floating away into the distance.

Deeper and deeper I swam, unable to see through the pitch black of the water but feeling unafraid. I belonged. I finally felt my body graze against the ocean floor and I sighed in contentment. This is where I was supposed to be.

Follow us...

I strained my eyes in the darkness to see the source of the playful voices, eager to understand my place here.

'Where are you?' I called.

An ethereal, glowing white figure appeared in front of me, her hair white and flowing all the way down to the end of her tail.

Tail? A moment of hesitation came over me. What kind of creature was this?

Before I could question it any further, her beautiful voice rippled across the waves to me.

Kaimana, Queen of the sea, join us…

I felt warm and happy. I swam toward her and followed her as she turned. She led me to a cave filled with more of her kind. I was in awe of their beauty and felt myself being drawn in further.

They all sweetly sang my name and welcomed me with open arms. Maybe Cyrus was right about my lineage. Maybe I was one of these creatures, too.

Cyrus… The name sparked something in the back of my mind and I shook my head. I was supposed to be finding Cyrus.

The tailed creature grabbed hold of my arm, and her nails left indentations in my skin.

'What are you doing?' I asked. 'I need to go.'

'You aren't going, Kaimana,' the creatures hissed in unison, with a sudden fearsomeness.

I seemed to awake from whatever stupor I had been put under and wrenched my arm away. The creatures were not beautiful. In fact, they were horrifying.

They were about 7ft in length, murky grey and their skin appeared to be falling away from their bones. The scales on their tails were rotten and torn, and their faces were gaunt. Fanged, bared teeth flashed at me from all around and several swipes of disgustingly long nails came toward me.

I spun around in panic and saw them all closing in on me. I was surrounded.

I tried to harness the water around me to throw them backward, but found it wouldn't move to my will. Their voices rang in my mind again.

We control the black sea…

I cried in pain as several claws raked at my skin and my blood created a cloud in the water. The skirt of my dress tore on all sides, several large chunks of fabric being ripped from the seams. Their touch sent a harrowing coldness through my bones. The scratch of their nails tore at me unrelentingly, and the pain grew as the same areas of my skin were clawed at repeatedly.

I used all the strength of my element to propel my swimming with enough force to blast through the growing crowd. They shrieked manically and lunged after me, scraping at my ankles as I kicked wildly. I swam in the direction I thought was up, but in the darkness I couldn't tell where I was really heading to.

One of them grabbed hold of my foot with a vice grip and pulled me backward, hard. I kicked it sharply in the face and it let out a wail. A chorus of hissing began as they closed in on me again and just as they caught up to my sides, reaching out to my arms, I breached the surface

and swam desperately to a shallower point where I could
stand.

The second my feet hit the floor, I pelted into a run, not
before one of them managed to graze my calf with their
teeth, a vicious parting gift that caused pain to blaze
through my leg and up my side, almost overwhelming
me.

As the water descended into the shore, they fell away and
sunk back below the water line, invisible once more. I
threw myself on to the beach and panted, gasping as the
pain from my missing flesh wracked through me.

I hobbled further up the beach and desperately looked
for Cyrus. If they had tricked him too, he would be dead.
'Cyrus!' I bellowed.

No answer. I forced myself to jog, grimacing through the
pain and circling around the outskirts of the cave for any
sight of him. Real panic crept in as I still saw no sign of
him. I ran back through the concealment spell and called
his name down the cave passage. No answer.

Tears escaped my eyes and travelled down my bloody
face as I began thinking he had to be dead. There was no
way he could swim strong enough to escape. I ran as fast
as my legs could bear, back to Zephyr.

'Where is he?' I pleaded.

Zephyr's already white eyes seemed to have glazed over
even more.

'Betrayal will prevail. The forgotten man will become
your saviour. Beware the shadows painted in smiles.
Blood is not stronger than water. Watch yours spill as you

save the condemned. The true leader will be unmasked,'
he recited monotonously, in a trance like state.

'What? Zephyr, snap out of it! Where is Cyrus?' I cried.
He did not seem to hear me and only repeated his words
over and over again. My heart raced, and I limped back
outside, my limbs weary and giving up.

'Cyrus...' I called, feeling woozy and my vision spotting
with white dots.

I heard a faint shuffling noise to my right and tried to
focus my vision. I began spinning water at my fingertips,
ready for whatever creature lay in wait.

'Kaia...,' a familiar voice croaked.

I gasped and found the strength to run to him
immediately.

'Cyrus!' I cried, falling to my knees beside him and
grasping him tightly. 'What happened? Are you okay?'

'Heard my name...something attacked...' he got out,
gesturing to his legs, which were torn to shreds.

'Oh, my god. Cyrus, heal yourself. Now!' I demanded.
His face was paling by the second and even through the
darkness of the night sky I could see the trail of blood
that had followed him in the sand.

He shook his head and through half open eyes looked at
the lacerations on my arms and face. He tried lifting his
hand up toward them.

'No,' I snapped, and retreated out of his reach.

I grabbed his hand and pressed it tightly to his legs. A
white glow began shining from them instantly, though it
seemed to dip in and out along with his consciousness.

Finally, the blood stopped pouring, and he was able to keep his hand there himself.

'What happened to you? You need healing,' he choked.

'You're far worse off than I am,' I replied as steadily as I could manage in an attempt to reassure him, and myself, that I would be okay.

His healing magic stopped, and he stood shakily on his feet.

I offered him my shoulder and clutched his waist, a reversal of our previous escape from his home, and we made our way back to the cave. I sat him down a short distance from Zephyr's prison, who was still in a trance.

'What attacked you?' I asked. 'Was it the mermaids?'

'Mermaids? No. It looked like a young child and I went to help it, it was calling out to me…' he said wistfully.

'They're trying to drive you from the island,' Zephyr suddenly interjected. 'I have heard the creatures many times trying to lure me away, but I've been unable to follow.'

I stood up quickly, too quickly that I wobbled on my feet and my vision blurred again.

'She needs healing,' said Zephyr. 'There's poison in her system.'

'I can't! She made me heal my legs!' Cyrus said desperately.

I could barely pay attention to their conversation and I slid back to the floor and tried to focus on my breathing.

'She can do it herself,' Zephyr instructed. 'She can draw on your power from the crystal.'

Cyrus hurried over and held my hand to my ankle where I had been bitten. I noticed, in a bleary state, that my veins were slowly turning black like the dark sea.

'Come on, Kaia. Focus on my energy, use the power,' Cyrus implored.

I tried to focus and feel his energy, but all I felt was an overwhelming tiredness.

'Come on!' he shouted.

I strained to focus my mind and felt a morsel of his energy intertwined with mine. I tried to imagine the glowing light that I had already seen so many times, and closed my eyes.

I couldn't tell if it was working or not until Cyrus breathed a sigh of relief.

I slowly felt my senses coming back to me and my eyes fluttered open to see his face right in front of mine, his eyes threatening to spill the tears that sat inside them.

'I thought you were dead,' I started.

'I know,' he shushed me. 'It's the least I deserve at this point.'

'No, that's not what I'm saying,' I interrupted, needing him to understand. 'I thought you were dead, and I didn't care anymore about what you did. I probably would have done the same,' I admitted. 'But I need to know when you released it, truthfully,' I explained to him in a weak voice, pushing myself to sit upright.

'I released it the moment we left your district. I swear to you.'

I nodded. That meant everything I had felt since the moment we left was true, and everything before…well, I didn't know.

'I forgive you,' I said. 'But do anything like that again and I'll kill you.'

He let out a surprisingly light laughter that I had never heard from him before.

'You have my word,' he spoke into my hair as he kissed my head, and despite both of us being on the brink of death, I felt content.

I turned to Zephyr, remembering what had happened to him.

'What were you reciting?' I asked.

Cyrus looked between us both, frowning, but I didn't have the energy to explain.

'It was a prophecy gifted to me by the stars. I was not given the answers that pair with it, however,' he answered.

I tipped my head back against the wall and nodded. 'Okay.'

My energy finally waned and I could not question him further. My eyes drifted closed, and I unwillingly drifted into a deep sleep.

Chapter 16

I awoke to the sound of Cyrus and Zephyr deep in
conversation. The previous night's events came to the
forefront of my mind, and I found myself not feeling so
forgiving over Cyrus' betrayal. The high stakes and
adrenaline filled panic had taken over any other feeling,
and although I didn't want Cyrus dead, I wasn't feeling so
fond of him either. I had decided to keep this to myself,
however, as I had already declared that I had forgiven
him and I didn't want to appear hypocritical.
I stretched and my limbs ached. My head felt clearer and
my thoughts were able to rationalise better than they had.
I noticed the veins, which were once black, were now
completely invisible again, and I sighed a breath of relief.

'...so where we would usually enter is completely patrolled
by guards,' Cyrus' voice rang out, 'and I would be
recognised immediately. Can you see whether a
concealment spell would work?'

'Dear boy, how many times must I say it? I cannot tell you everything I see, for it will cause an entirely different outcome,' Zephyr replied wearily.

Cyrus groaned.

Where we usually enter. The phrase stuck in my mind. It had never occurred to me that, in fact, Cyrus had been to The Centre before with his family.

'You've been inside?' I asked him.

'Me and my family have spent some time here, though not as much as the Asturias' or the Grendafiels. Generally, they like to keep us and the Arexias in the districts. When the district is less powerful, they require less watching over, less directing. So I don't know it as well as you might assume.'

'So what *have* you seen?' I pressed.

'Honestly? It's really hard to remember. Nine times out of the ten that my father went, he would leave me behind. He would say it was good practice for me to be alone as a ruler. All I can really recall is passing through the gates, and a general map out of the buildings in the courtyard,' Cyrus said, his eyes scrunching as he tried to remember.

'The courtyard?' I asked.

'Imagine The Centre as a circle. Now, you have buildings, houses, prisons et cetera around the edge, right at the top of the circle, in line with Air, lives the High Priest. He rules The Centre, and essentially everything else too, as he also controls the district leaders. In front of the High Priest's mansion, there's a glorious fountain. There's a real mermaid imbued in the stone who sings in the most mesmerising voice.'

I shuddered at the mention of mermaids; they were certainly not mesmerising once you were in their grasp. 'How did they capture it?' I asked.

Cyrus shrugged and turned to Zephyr.

'Well, you probably know,' he said. 'Or can you not tell us that, either?'

Zephyr chuckled and said, 'That I can tell you. When my magic was stolen and the districts were formed, each was given a defence designed to keep fae out, and also to keep them in. Now, of course, like any true dictator, there needed to be a place for himself and the upper class fae to reside, away from the low borns, and so The Centre was fractured away from the districts. The defences for the island weren't quite so extravagant as those of the districts. They were more subtle. The upper class did not want to have an eye sore outside of their homes. The sea surrounding us turned a deadly black, the beaches covered in corpses and the towering mountains unreachable. In a place so desolate, only demonic creatures of the night could survive. They slowly took over the area, and were mostly left that way as a precaution, in case anyone slipped through the cracks. Fae who lived in The Centre were, and still are, brimming with arrogance, sure they could do as they pleased and take what they wanted. A group of pirates sailed from The Centre and were sure they could pillage the districts. Of course, they barely made it a mile out before the mermaids claimed their souls. Instead of using this as a teaching lesson that fae could not, in fact, overpower the natural order, a large group of officers were sent on a mission to retrieve one of these mermaids and bring her back to the island. Many lost their lives, and it was a dreadful day for so many families, but unfortunately, they did manage to capture one who appeared to have been a child. She was magically strung up onto the fountain and an enchantment keeps her singing day and night. As she grew, her limbs became one with the stone that holds her, and she will remain there until she dies, most likely about 200 years from now. I can see her in my mind's eye. She sings so sweetly, and looks so beautiful, but her eyes are full of torment, and her body looks no better than that of a skeleton.'

Despite my recent interaction with her kind, I couldn't help but feel sympathy for her. She was just a child, essentially tortured all these years and would be for many, many more.

'I do find it bold that he has declared himself as the High Priest,' Zephyr said. 'However, the audacity of his ego does not surprise me.'

'Who?' I asked.

'The cloaked fae who stole my magic and created this turmoil. It is he who rules Elorial. If he had died, the magic would have reverted to me instantly, and I would no longer be here.'

'So the High Priest is also the figure in your vision who killed your daughter?' Cyrus clarified.

'One and the same,' Zephyr said grimly.

A silence descended upon us all and you could practically feel the atmosphere plummet into darkness. A loud growl from my stomach interrupted the silence, and I was grateful for the distraction. I realised I had still not eaten. 'I'm going to head out and try to find some food. We're all starved,' I said, hoping it hadn't sounded like an ironic joke to Zephyr.

'I'll help,' said Cyrus, following me out of the cave passage and through the hidden entrance.

We walked in silence for a long while, occasionally kicking the sand to look for shellfish, or stopping at a wiry plant to check for any berries.

'Do you even know what plants would be safe to eat?' I asked him.

'Pretty much. Well, I know which ones we can't eat, anyway.'

I nodded awkwardly and carried on scouring for any change in the environment. Without our usual back and forth bickering, there was an awfully different feeling between us.

'Can we just move past...' I began.

'I wanted to apologise again for...' he said at the very same time.

I blew out a breath of air and waited for him to continue.

'Sorry. I just wanted to apologise again for not telling you sooner about what I did. I knew you'd get worked up, and I just didn't want it to affect our mission. But I appreciate you forgiving me and I'm glad you see my point of view,' he said.

I stopped dead and felt a hard hit of disbelief slap on to my features. That wasn't much of an apology at all.

Cyrus looked at me, his brows pressed together slightly and his smooth brown eyes moving back and forth across my face.

'You're apologising for not telling me?' I clarified.

'Yes.'

'And your justification is that I would get *worked up* and ruin our mission?' I asked again, my voice rising.

'Yes.'

'And you don't see where the problem lies in that *apology*?'

'No?' he replied, as though I had said something absurd. 'You said that you forgive me, so I don't need to apologise for that. But I thought I would do the decent thing and show my regret for the rest of it.'

I sputtered out a laugh in shock, and continued walking straight past him. I heard him muttering to himself behind me and called back to him, 'You know, sometimes people can say they forgive you, but not really mean it yet! You're not supposed to keep rubbing salt in the wound by being an *ass.*'

'Well, why would you say it if you didn't really mean it?' he asked in surprise.

'Because you almost *died*, Cyrus. I had other things on my mind!'

He said nothing and walked a few paces behind me. I wanted to completely ignore him until he realised how arrogant he was being, but unfortunately, that would most likely take us weeks. Instead, I settled for only granting him one syllable responses, and refusing to discuss the situation any further - the *mature* way.

We had circled the entire way around the island without finding a morsel to eat. My stomach was growling in protest and my ribs were aching. I laid down on the sand in the sun, unable to help but wonder if this is where we would die. Cyrus dropped next to me and unbuttoned his shirt, leaving his torso to glisten in the sun. We sat there for a long while, resting in silence and contemplating what was to come. I appreciated that these may be our last ever moments of freedom and relative peace.

Cyrus messed around, flicking flames at patches on the sand and watching them fizzle out. He did this for ten minutes or so, when something caught my eye.

'Do that again,' I said urgently to him.

He frowned and flicked a flame in front of me, and I watched intently.

Yes!

I laughed in delight as I pointed at where the burnt sand now laid. He looked at me, a concerned expression on his face, which for some reason reminded me of Paula, and I had to drop my gaze to stop myself from spiraling in longing to see her.

I cleared my throat, my mood severely dampened, and shoved my fingers into the burning hot sand. When they emerged, they held a small, wriggling insect.

Cyrus gasped and did it again, this time pulling one out for himself.

'This whole beach is filled with them,' he whispered.

We set to work, him firing flames and me digging for creatures. I ripped off what remained of my skirt and used it as a makeshift bag, and eventually we filled it with the disgusting, creepy things. Beggars could not be choosers.

We headed back to Zephyr, ready to feast.

Cyrus created a makeshift fire pit on the ground in front of Zephyr's prison, and I tipped the critters inside it. They ran in every direction, but were barricaded on all sides by large rocks. A few tiny ones slipped through the cracks, but they weren't what we were after anyway, so we let them wiggle away to freedom.

Cyrus flicked a finger and set them ablaze. I couldn't help but feel slightly guilty, but my stomach grumbled at me again and my remorse evaporated.

We divided them three ways, despite Zephyr's constant protests.

'I don't need to eat, child. I will live for many more years to come with this spell upon me. You will not if you don't eat what you have,' he argued.

I ignored him completely and pressed a handful of fried insects into his palm.

Me and Cyrus ate immediately. The bugs were crunchy and squelchy, but provided the most relief my body had ever felt. I scoffed them down quickly, craving the sustenance, and I noticed Cyrus did the same.

I turned to Zephyr, interested to see his reaction as he gingerly placed one upon his dry tongue. He chewed it slowly, swallowed…and was then violently sick.

I watched in horror as stomach acid covered the perfectly good food and tried not to groan aloud.

'Are you okay?' I asked once he had finally stopped.

'Yes. My body is not accustomed to digestion of insects, or anything at all for that matter. It's for the best,' Zephyr sighed, 'It would only have triggered hunger pangs again and that is a great nuisance I could do without.'

I pursed my lips and was about to apologise for making him try one, when his face morphed into horror and his hand stretched out of the iron bars.

'Zephyr! What is it?' Cyrus asked.

Zephyr wasn't able to speak, and waved his hand around urgently. We both clutched it at the same time, Cyrus' hand sitting on top of mine, and saw through the eye in Zephyr's mind.

'Ladies and gentlefae, thank you for attending this ceremonial event!' a hooded figure boomed. 'Today we have TWO traitors, ready to be executed after being tried for their crimes!'

The crowd roared, and a wave of applause began.

'Yes, yes. Now first, let's bring out the fae who led us to these heathens!'

Two fae, one female and one male, walked out onto the heightened stage.

'Here we have with us, Mario De'Larin and Jazlean King!' the figure cried, gesturing toward the two fae that stood uncomfortably on the stage. 'When we asked the districts for information, these fae were the first to step up. They will be greatly rewarded for their service!'

They were ushered off of the stage to cheers and whoops of support from the crowd, and two more were brought on, their heads covered by hoods.

'Now, as you know, these fae were known conspirators of the treacherous Kaimana Green and Cyril Ramos! Today, they will say their final words and be sentenced to death for treason. Unmask them.'

The hoods were pulled off and two fae were revealed. One dark haired boy with a large scar down his cheek, and one older lady with a white streak running through her hair.

'Darin Versyl and Paula Groff, any last words to your criminal associates?' the cloaked man asked.

Darin pleaded for this life, insisting he knew nothing, but was cut off by a winding vine snaking around him and slitting his throat.

Paula looked around in fear, and finally spoke in a trembling voice, 'I don't know what you've got yourself into, duck, but I hope you...'

Her words were cut off and replaced by screams as her body became alight. Silence fell as the flames burned away every trace of her, and then the crowd roared once more.

Hundreds of fae all rushed toward the stage, jeering and cheering for their leader.

Prisoners lined up in the iron cages remained silent, stone faced and dejected. Hundreds of them stood imprisoned, separated by element. In Earth, there stood several dark haired fae, all on the larger side except for one particularly skinny girl. In Water, there were less fae, mostly silver haired except for one red haired woman and a few golden haired men. In Fire, there stood the most prisoners of them all. All dark haired and olive toned skin, their faces looking the most rebellious of them all. And in Air, the

*least populated prison, fair haired and pale skinned fae stood
beside one another, all of them men.
The crowd was shushed and the cloaked leader began announcing
more news to the ever growing crowd.*

Cyrus held my hand in a death grip, and immediately
placed his other hand on my shoulder.

'Wasn't that your boss? They had one sacrifice for each of
us…' he continued talking, but his voice faded away into
the background.

'Is that the future?' I asked Zephyr quietly.

'Yes,' he said. 'But Kaimana, you must know, not all my
visions are years ahead. This one is going to come into
play in a few short moments.'

'You can't know that,' I whispered.

'I know all,' he replied gravely.

I dropped to my knees and screamed. I screamed so
loudly Cyrus was forced to cover his ears instead of
attempting to console me. Even Zephyr made a face of
discomfort, but I didn't care.

Because of me, Paula was dead.

Chapter 17

I didn't know how much time had passed. It might have been an hour, it might have been a day. I was trapped in a torturous prison inside my mind. And I didn't want to leave.

I wanted to feel every ounce of pain, hurt and suffering; it was still nothing compared to what Paula must have felt when she was burned alive.

I sat on the floor, unmoving, while Cyrus and Zephyr continued to talk. Cyrus often tried to talk to me, to ask me more about who she was and how I was feeling. I suppose it had looked strange. I was in a state of complete and total despair, but not a single tear had escaped my eye. Zephyr would then eventually call him off when I would remain mute.

I couldn't stop replaying her words in my head.

I don't know what you've gotten yourself into, duck, but I hope you… Screams.

Even on her deathbed, she remained affectionate toward me. What had she hoped? Hoped I succeeded? Hoped I stopped and returned home? I didn't know, and it didn't matter. She would never speak again to be able to tell me. I sat for an even longer time. Cyrus was in and out of the cave, doing whatever he was doing, and Zephyr stayed very quiet. My limbs ached in stiffness and my spine was bruised from my leaning against the rough wall, but I didn't move. Not until the emotional exhaustion took over me and led me into a fitful sleep.

It took an exceptional amount of time to be able to drift into unconsciousness. It could hardly be called rest - I spent the entire time reliving Paula's death, my parents being brutally attacked and seeing myself covered in the blood of those I loved. The thing about nightmares is they're supposed to be imaginary. You wake up, and the big, bad monster disappears and you realise it was all a dream. Well, when I awoke, I was the monster, and all of it was real.

'...she needs a little more time. She should come round today,' said Zephyr in a hushed voice.

'I still don't understand. Why does she care so much?' asked Cyrus.

'It's not for me to tell, Cyrus.'

Cyrus sighed and sat back down against the wall.

'Why did you show us that?' I asked Zephyr, making Cyrus jump in surprise.

'Kaimana, I need to know if you saw what I saw…' Cyrus began to prattle.

I shot him a withering look and turned back to Zephyr.

'Why did you show us that?' I asked again, more slowly this time.

'I know it was an unbearable thing to see,' he sighed, 'but unfortunately, it is essential to your journey for you to know the truth. You are being spoken about all over Elorial. No one has ever escaped their districts and lived to tell the tale.'

'So why haven't they said we're dead?' I asked. Although, I didn't really feel like I could bring myself to truly care.

'They can't. You were sighted in Fire. Either way, people know you escaped the Water district successfully.'

'Why did they call him Cyril Ramos?'

'We don't know,' Cyrus said, diverting my attention. 'But we suspect it's because they can't let people know an heir has gone rogue. Likelihood is, if I was caught, they would kill me and blame it on a tragic accident, and not tarnish my family line.'

I thought of the cloaked fae. The hooded figure that caused this never ending circuit of pain and suffering. I felt murderous rage grab ahold of my heart, and I jumped to my feet.

Cyrus watched me warily.

'Let's go,' I said.

'Go?' Cyrus asked.

'Yes. Let's go. We know how to get into The Centre, we know where to go for the prisoners and I'm sure it won't take much to figure out where the Asturias' are. You deal with them and get your brother, and I'll kill the cloaked fae.'

'How you intend to fight someone with the powers of the original zodiacs?' asked Zephyr.

I had no idea how I intended to fight him, but I wasn't going to sit here nibbling on insects any longer.

'Why don't you capitalise on the fact you are in the presence of a fae directly descended from Apollo?' he suggested.

I looked at Cyrus hungrily, ready to fight.

'Outside,' I barked.

We walked side by side, out onto the beach. I gestured for him to step in front of me beside the water and settled into a fighting stance.

'I don't really know that this is going to be overly helpful…' Cyrus began to say.

'Go!' I called.

I could not draw on the water at our feet - as the mermaids had said, they controlled the black sea - so I had to use the elemental power that lived inside of me. I took a deep breath and as I exhaled, allowed powerful jets of water to shoot rapidly from all over my body. Working in a thunderous beat, they fired relentlessly as I kept my eyes trained on Cyrus' hands. He shot streams of fire as soon as the water neared him, fizzling them to steam. I changed my tactic and focused the jets into one singular form. I made it take the shape of a sea snake and sent it slithering toward him. He directed his flames at its head, but my snake was far too quick and nimble for that. It jerked to the side, coiled, and sprung. Its jaws spread open wide, wide enough to engulf Cyrus' entire body. He threw flames out left and right, but didn't manage to hit my snake's writhing body. I allowed him to eat Cyrus, before dropping the water completely and letting it splash to the ground. Cyrus stood there, soaked and scowling. 'You aren't fighting me properly,' I said. 'Use your dark flames.'

'No,' he said firmly. 'I can't control them well enough.'

'What better way to prepare me? You once said that learning dark magic gives you an edge over your opponent. Well, personally, I think the even better edge to have is knowing how to defeat dark magic.'

'I'm stopping if I feel even an ounce of myself slipping.'

I nodded and braced. I had no idea how I had won against his dark magic that day in no-man's land.

Black flames rose from his palms, encircled his body and flashed with runic symbols.

The energy from my amethyst connected to me instantly, as naturally as breathing, and I used it to begin attempting to break Cyrus' protective cage of flames. I tried quick fire, constant pressure, larger quantities and even to wrap a tentacle the whole way around the heat, but to no avail. I was beginning to tire, and knew I was running low on power. I glanced around, wondering if I could utilise any debris, when my eyes fell to the black sea yet again.

I closed my eyes and took a steadying breath before draining every last drop of my power into harnessing the sea. I felt a pushing and pulling sensation on my magic and wondered if I was actually engaging in a fight for power with the mermaids as opposed to the water itself. I felt a warm sensation spread through me, and knew the parts of Cyrus' magic that laid inside my amethyst were now aiding me as well. With a roar of determination, I finally managed to lift a tentacle of pure black water out from the shoreline. I opened my eyes and watched it gleefully, then set my sights on Cyrus. I could see his face flickering through the flames every now and again, and he looked astounded.

Now I had control of this part of the water, it was easy to manipulate. I sent it to the top of Cyrus' black flames, and I saw him reinforce his defence as I did so. I simply pushed the tentacle down on top of them. It took a great deal of exertion and I knew I was going to be drained for hours after this, but I carried on regardless. The shades of black swirled together and where the flames met the water, a grey smoke followed. My water was slowly sizzling out, but not quicker than Cyrus' flames were being extinguished. I pushed down and down, feeling as though I were trying to push a building along with my bare hands, and eventually the water crashed to the floor, and the black flames were gone.

I grinned at Cyrus, and his expression of shock still did not waver.

'How did you do that?' he asked.

I shrugged and plopped onto the floor, feeling weak but victorious. We both laid back on the sand, absorbing the heat of the sun.

I felt a sense of victory that I had managed to achieve such a feat. Here I was, surrounded by dark magic and fighting against one of the most powerful fae of my time, and I *won*.

It made me think back to Cyrus' remark that I came from powerful lineage, and seriously wondered if it could be true.

A few moments later, Cyrus finally spoke. 'Who was she to you?'

I sighed and my reflexes told me to shut this conversation down immediately, but I knew Cyrus would not stop asking, so I chose to give him just enough information than I previously had done to quash his interest.

'She was my boss. You saw her briefly back in Water. But she was much more than that,' I said. 'When I was young and my parents died, I began spending a lot of time at the library. It was quiet and I could escape everyone else who believed I was a traitor. She noticed me and spent time with me. I was only six years old, and she cared for me like I was her own. She would bring in meals for me when my foster parents didn't feed me, knit me blankets and jumpers, and let me stay hours past closing to avoid going home. As I grew, she gave me a job, and I spent every day with her. She came to the district hall to fight my case to have my own property, and then helped me to move there. Even as an adult, she would bring me food, clothes, anything I needed. We spent everyday together, and she had nothing but love for everyone around her. She was the mother and the best friend I never had.'

Cyrus reached over and gripped my hand tightly in comfort.

'I knew the boy,' he said quietly. 'He was my best friend when we were young. I used to escape and play with him whenever I could, and he knew all about the terrible treatment me and my mother received at the hands of my father. We stopped talking about six years ago, when I turned 14. My responsibilities were piling up too high, and honestly, I became arrogant. I didn't believe I needed lower born friends. I don't know why he was handed in as a conspirator. We haven't spoken in years.'

I said nothing, as there was nothing to say. There were no words of comfort or reassurances that could be made.

I thought back to the vision and realised in my all consuming grief I had forgotten who had turned Paula over in the first place. Jazlean King.

I felt a spitting fury course through my veins, and the image of her face in my mind brought back the murderous rage I had been feeling before. Paula had not known a single thing. I had lied to her for months in order to protect her, and that venomous bitch had turned her over for nothing more than to spite me.

'I need to know if you saw what I saw,' Cyrus said, interrupting my thoughts.

'What?'

'We saw the prisoners, right? Well, one of them was the woman from the vision I saw when you entered no-man's land that day. The red haired woman? She looked thinner, and more worn, but I would place my life on the fact it was her.'

I sat bolt upright. My mother? How did I miss that? I tried desperately to think back to what we had seen, but only remembered a vague image of someone with red hair, not her face. Even so, how many red haired water residents were there? Hardly any.

'My parents are in there,' I whispered.

We had eventually gone back inside after Cyrus collected more insects for us to eat.

Me and Cyrus ate quietly, and Zephyr sat as he always did, cross-legged and hunched over. I scoured our surroundings. We would soon be leaving this place that had provided us temporary safety, but I knew we would be coming back.

'I will come back for you,' I said to Zephyr.

He tutted and shook his head. 'I am unimportant in the larger picture, Kaimana. Focus on what you truly need to achieve.'

'I will. But either way, I will return with the High Priest's head, and the magic to free you.'

He smiled softly and didn't argue any further.

'Why are the Leo and Pisces bones important for us?' I asked him, recalling how he had been so concerned about whether we had them when we arrived.

'They will play a vital part in your battle with the cloaked fae. He holds the power of Aries, and so you will require your own ancestral power in order to level the playing field. Of course, he has access to all four elements also, though he doesn't use them in the public eye, so you will still be out matched,' he answered.

'But Cyrus is the descendant, not me.'

'This is true, but do you not think it odd that you are able to break through dark magic? Ishtar was the goddess of the Pisces. She was a god of love, fertility, and life. But she was also a goddess of war. Her powers were almighty, but contradictory. She created chaos and order, love and violence. Does that not sound like you?' he said.

It sounded exactly like me. For every face I had, another lurked beneath it, the complete opposite. I craved order, control, and yet chaos followed me like the plague. Me and Cyrus were a relationship born of violence, slowly morphing into…

I didn't finish that thought as it headed toward a place I didn't want to explore.

'But she's not my ancestor,' I said, still confused.

'The sign of the Pisces is the most complicated of them all. You hold traits of each of the zodiacs, and this means many planetary rulers play a part in your power. That does not mean you are descended from them all, it simply means your power is in tune with them. For that reason, you will want the power source of Ishtar to aid you.'

I still wasn't sure I followed. Zephyr always seemed to speak in riddles, and never gave a clear cut answer to anything, but I dropped the topic, anyway.

I noticed Cyrus was extremely quiet, and I kept stealing glances when he wasn't looking, trying to read his expressions. He seemed detached somehow, like he wasn't really here.

Zephyr expelled a deep sigh and shook his head.

'What is it?' I asked.

He said nothing and just continued shaking his head.

Cyrus looked at him warily, and then turned to me.

'Let's go and get some more food,' he said.

'Okay,' I agreed, still hungry anyway and grateful for this menial task, when so much more seemed to loom ahead of us.

We headed out onto the beach and walked along under the sunset for a while before settling down in a spot to insect - hunt. Rain pattered down on top of us and I welcomed the embrace of water.

'I would destroy anyone that hurt you,' Cyrus said quietly. 'You know that?'

I didn't answer. I wasn't sure I did know that. He seemed to have affection for me, but he could be so misleading.

'From the first time I saw you, I thought it. I couldn't bare any vulnerability to you, though. You're ruthless,' he chuckled. 'I watched as you slept in Water, simply overwhelmed by your existence. You would awake the next day and spit sass at me and I would bite back, but inside, I loved it. I craved our relentless arguing. For that reason, I thought I was no good for you. I was a monster of chaos, but I soon realised, so were you. We're like two atoms, spinning and whizzing around one another, occasionally colliding but never straying from our path. Drawn to one another, no matter how much it hurts. When my father spoke of you in that way,' - he shuddered-, 'I thought I was going to kill him there and then. I tell you this because I'm not sure that both of us will make it through this, and I would die a regretful man if I didn't tell you of your beauty, so radiant that you put even the sun to shame. Your admirable determination, no matter how bleak our situation. You would make a fine ruler. I don't know if you feel the same, but if we come out of this alive, I want you. I want you now and forever, always.'

My heart raced, and I felt as though my soul were singing. We had been everything. Enemies, tolerated by one another, to allies, to…this. I had spent so much time in painful denial because I couldn't be sure that he wasn't out to hurt me. But time and time again, he had bared his truth to me in a way that was so vulnerable, and it had been me who did not give him the same back.

'I spent a long time thinking I couldn't trust you. That you were just using me for what you needed. I didn't ever stop to think that that could be true, but so could everything else. All the words of desire you've spoken to me, I only let myself believe you used them as a means of manipulation, without considering you might feel just as stuck as I did,' I said.

Cyrus brushed his hand across my cheek and then fastened it in my hair. I felt swirling butterflies in my stomach and finally gave in to my wants. I wanted him.

'Now and forever, always,' I whispered.

We locked eyes and something seemed to come ablaze between us. Every part of my body was electrified, and I felt like we had merged into one being. His pain was mine, his happiness was mine, and his love.

He leant in and my heart skipped a beat. At long last, after months of our back and forth, his lips pressed against mine.

Fireworks seemed to explode in my gut. I clutched onto his arm and melted against the softness of his kiss.

The rain fell all around us and trapped us in the moment. Pure happiness washed over me and I sunk even further into his embrace.

He eventually pulled back, and I opened my eyes. He had tears streaming from his eyes and his lips were trembling fiercely.

I frowned as I tried to figure out what could possibly be wrong in this long awaited moment, and then I felt it.

A warm, sharp feeling in my stomach. I gasped and dropped my hand to the source of the pain. I looked down, my hand slick with blood, and Cyrus holding the hilt of his golden dagger which was stabbed into my abdomen.

'I'm so sorry,' he wept. 'I'm so sorry, Kaimana. But we were born in violence and it was always going to end that way.'

He shakily pulled the dagger from my stomach and words failed me as the pain ricocheted through my body.

I heard him sob and stand up. I fell backwards onto the sand, my vision blurring. The last thing I saw was his back walking away from me, and the rain washing my blood down the beach.

Then it went dark.

Printed in Great Britain
by Amazon